To my dear friend, Sandy.

Always there for me, listening and encouraging. I will miss her so very much, especially her sense of humour and lovely smile.

Contents

STATION INFORMATION
Salisbury
South Western Railway
Wide gate
4
and collect
tickets here

1:

Hatching the Plan

"Oh, hi Sandy, so lovely to hear from you, what have you been up to these past few weeks?" said Anna, munching on an apple whilst juggling the home phone with her left hand, managing to scrunch it up to her ear whilst still holding onto the apple.

"Hi Anna, what are you eating girl it sounds like a pony munching on a carrot!"

Anna chuckled, nearly choking herself in the process, and screwed up her face in merriment.

"Not far off old friend, just eating an apple as it happens."

Sandy made a resigned face at the phone and then went on, "I'm just phoning to see if you'd be able to come with me to Devon next week for a few days? I have booked a little holiday cottage and was going with my sister-in-law, but she's just let me know that she's decided to go to Spain with her daughter instead! Well thanks a bunch for that, I thought in my head, but I really didn't blame her, I know which one I would prefer if I had the choice." Anna went a little quiet and her brain started to chug into some sort of action… hum, next week? What was going on at work, and could she get the time off at such short notice? Her boss Graham was pretty understanding, and she really didn't have a lot on at the moment, so that should be achievable.

"Hi Sand, are you there? Oh good, well yes, I think that would be ok as I think I can swing the time off work as next week doesn't seem too busy. It will be good to have an adventure together as we haven't done that in a long time, and we can natter till our hearts' content for five days, which shouldn't be difficult for us!"

"Brilliant news, said Sandy, I'll just book the rail tickets and will send you a confirmation email.

I'll see you next Tuesday then for our mini-adventure, dum, de, dum dum, dahhhh!"

Anna could hear Sandy chuckling to herself - her friend was completely nuts but she loved her to bits and they had been good friends now for over forty years!

"Umm what are you going to bring as I will need my dressing gown, slippers, own bread, jam, own spread, biscuits, tea, coffee, milk, walking shoes and boots, just to name but a few!"

Anna had been holding the phone away from her ear on speaker as she knew exactly what Sandy would take and the suitcase would be humungous, with enough food for an army on the march in the middle of an arctic winter!

"Oh yes, Sandy I know! By the way, who, by all that is holy, is going to scoff all that food as we could actually donate it to the third world." This was said with much affection as she knew that Sandy always catered for EVERY EVENTUALITY including a nuclear war, or an alien invasion!

"That will be fine and I will bring the chocolates and cakes, ha, ha."

They both ended the conversation in high spirits with much giggling like teenagers even though they were both in their sixty's. How come it did not feel like that?

159 015

happen and after a good 10 to15 minutes they started to trundle their cases off the platform and down a steep slope. This was no mean feat as the huge raving looney monster case had a mind of its own and kept veering off to the side, pulling both women after it. Anna eventually had to walk in front to 'steer' the wayward beast until, eventually, after about half a mile they came out in front of a small café. There was no taxi to be seen and, after waiting for 10 minutes, they rang the number on the taxi firm's card. Apparently the driver had been and gone as he had not waited once the train had left the station! Really? So, after a slightly heated altercation, he agreed to come back to pick them up. Eventually, the taxi arrived and Anna and Sandy scrambled in with the driver grumbling and asking, "I suppose you want them cases in the boot?"

Then proceeded to grumble about the weight of the cases and how some people had no idea how bad his back was and why did they come on holiday anyway, as he, to be fair, heaved the bulging cases in the back of the car. When he asked for the address of the holiday cottage he was, again, not amused and on arriving at the Holiday Park, said he could not take them to the cottage, as it could be anywhere and they would have to walk the rest of the way! Added to this he charged them double the rate and zoomed off in a cloud of dirty diesel fumes. Well, what a pleasant man, so polite and helpful, NOT!

However, despite everything, they had arrived! Not quite though as they had to find their cottage, chalet really, and after making enquiries, trundled their cases between them across a car park and up a slope, by which time they were both puffed out, to arrive at their destination, cold, out of breath and tired. The chalet looked really cozy and clean and so they tried to open the combination lock. Oh no! Whatever they tried it would not budge they obviously had all the right numbers but they had not necessarily been written down in the right order! Sandy just collapsed in a heap on her case and said she would not budge until morning and she would sleep where she sat! Anna phoned the number on the ticket and the owner answered, giving them the combination, this time in the right order, and at long last they opened the door and fell into the little hallway.

"Tea, tea and more tea! shouted Sandy and proceeded to fill the kettle and unearth the tea bags, sugar, milk and biscuits she had stashed in various places. You see, she grinned, all my supplies do come in handy in times of emergencies and much stress."

Anna could only agree with her and much later, they both sat with their shoes off and with much noises of great pleasure, greedily quaffed their precious tea.

Later, when they were both much refreshed, they started to investigate and found very pleasant accommodation. The little chalet had been newly refurbished and painted, was clean and airy with two pretty bedrooms.

"I'm bagging the double bed," said Sandy, diving into the room to her left and Anna had the twin room which was absolutely fine and meant she could use the other bed to lay out some of her clothes. Much later they went for a stroll down to the sea and realised it was a very pretty, if quaint, seafront with the old fashioned 'bucket and spade' brigade apparent. Here there were no modern fripperies but just a few shops, ice cream parlours and the sand and sea. Ideal for little families on a budget and it reminded Anna of her own childhood spent on golden beaches, running up and down the sand with buckets of water making sandcastles and just generally mucking about.

That first night they opted for a meal out in one of the beachside bars. They had fish and chips and ham, egg and chips, a nice glass of wine each and raising their glasses, made a toast to 'old friends and happy days'. That night they retired early and both hit the sack not stirring until the morning.

3:

Shifty Neighbour

The next morning the two friends made tea, had breakfast and decided to go and explore their surroundings. Anna pulled back the curtain to survey the little grassed courtyard with other chalets facing onto it in neat little rows. There was some activity but, as the weather looked pretty dismal and cold, not seasonal for June, there was only a brave few scurrying about or sitting on their little verandahs drinking their beverages. As Anna looked across the little green, a man emerged from the door of the chalet opposite. He was hunched over against the wind and rain, had a hat on and a mobile phone to his ear. He was in deep conversation with someone and even though she could not hear him, realised he was shouting down the phone and gesticulating fiercely with a scowl on his angular face. He did not look like a holiday-maker at all and she supposed that is why he caught her attention, that and the fact that he had a very pronounced limp. Oh well, it took all sorts she supposed and he may just be having a short break away from a stressful job or situation.

"Where are we going?" shouted Sandy and it brought Anna out of her daydream and back to reality.

"Wherever you want, flower," was her reply.

The two friends got themselves kitted out for the weather and decided they would catch a bus to the nearest big town and have a meander around the shops, a little light lunch and make their way leisurely back to the chalet. For the moment the shifty looking man opposite was forgotten in a flurry of activity to evacuate the little holiday let and explore.

"Crikey this wind is strong," said Sandy as they battled their way out of the complex and up to the bus stop.

"You don't say!" said Anna as the breath was caught and taken away from her by the sharp wind.

The rain was annoying but not too heavy, which was a good job, as they both had difficulty keeping their umbrellas skywards. As they got to the end of the path, Anna saw something glistening on the gravel and as they got nearer discovered it was a woman's lipstick case, the top of which was cracked and damaged. Anna picked it up and turned it around between her fingers. The owner would probably not want it back as it was covered in mud and broken but, what was clear, were the initials on the barrel of the case, being CD.

Just for the moment she pulled out a small plastic bag from her pocket and popped the lipstick into it, for what purpose really, she did not at this moment in time know, but thinking she might reunite it with its owner if they occupied one of the holiday lets nearby.

The two friends had a brilliant day and travelled into Torquay experiencing all the joys of bus travel. All sorts of people were on board some in wheelchairs, some with sticks, young people going to work and families with small children going to nearby attractions. The bus must have stopped so many times that it was a wonder it arrived at its destination on time! The noise of everyone's chatter and laughter was quite deafening and also quite infectious.

"The rich and famous should try this mode of transport someday and it might make them appreciate their privileged lifestyle of being chauffeured around or going by private jet" shouted Sandy over the chatter.

The rich tapestry of life was apparent all around and it was good to feel a part of this life and absorb the holiday atmosphere. They mooched round the shops and purchased a few bits and pieces, ending up in a department store where they had a good lunch, obviously still chatting furiously, and taking in the hustle and bustle of the restaurant. In the afternoon they walked along the seafront and bought an ice cream from one of the kiosks, sitting down on a wooden bench to enjoy it. At that precise moment the sun came out and it was so good to feel the heat on their faces whilst eating the cold, creamy ice cream. It felt like they were just two kids again, enjoying the moment, they could have been anywhere in the world for all they cared.

All too soon it was time to board the double-decker and head back to their little seaside haven. The journey back took a lot less time and there did not seem so many people to pick up at each stop.

They alighted and went in search of a takeaway for the evening meal. Once they had decided on their choice of meal they ordered, picked it up and trundled back home, or so it felt. They were both so tired after they had eaten their meal that, after baths and hair washing etc, they had a drink and fell into their respective beds, thoroughly exhausted but pleasantly so.

4:

Things That Go Bump in the Night!

Bang! Creak! Thud! Thud! Scrape…

Anna awoke with a start and could not, at first, gather her wits to think where she was. It took a little time to realise that she was in the little chalet and on holiday. Again she heard scraping and a dragging sound. Whatever was that? Gingerly she looked out of the curtains in her room but could see nothing. She put on her slippers and quietly opened her door to emerge into the little lounge-come-kitchen. There were no lights on and it had to be around 2 o'clock in the morning. Slowly she made her way to the windows and pulled the curtains back slightly. At first she could see nothing, as it was so dark, but then she saw a shadow moving, and yes, it was someone bending over and dragging a long object along the path opposite. The bundle must have been quite heavy as there were sounds coming from the person dragging it, being consistent with someone finding the task very difficult. As Anna continued to stare it became apparent that the person dragging the bundle was… yes, limping. Did that mean then, that it was the man she had seen this morning coming out of the let opposite? What was he dragging along the path at this time of night and where was he going? At that moment she felt a hand on her arm and jumped within an inch of her life, then realised that it was Sandy who had come to peer out of the window with her, presumably also having heard something. Anna put a finger to her mouth to signal not to make a sound and indicated that Sandy should watch with her. She was careful not to move the curtains too much and because they had no lights on in the chalet, was sure the man could not see them. He was furtively looking this way and that and his progress was slow. Eventually he disappeared around the corner of the end chalet and from there he would have to drag, whatever it was, over to the car park. They continued to stare out of the window but no-one appeared around the corner and all was again quiet and still. They watched for some time but he did not reappear.

The friends looked at each other and did not move for a little while. Anna whispered to Sandy not to put on a light but they both retired to Sandy's room at the back of the chalet to talk.

"What was all that about?" said Sandy when they had shut the door.

Anna knew that Sandy always had a small torch by the side of her bed and found it, switching it on. They both looked really spooky as the light illuminated their faces.

"I really, really, don't know, said Anna however, I am sure it does not look good unless there is a simple explanation as to why you'd drag something out of your hut at two in the morning and possibly deposit it in your car. What could it have been, and why would you do it in the middle of the night unless you had something to hide?"

"This is the time for a cup of tea," said Sandy and with the torch pointed firmly on the ground made her way to the kitchen, filling the kettle and putting it on to boil.

Once made, she carried two cups back to the bedroom and

they sat on her bed, sipping the amber liquid, both deep in contemplation and both slightly shivering with cold and nerves. They decided to sleep on it and Anna went back to her bedroom, wishing Sandy goodnight, and surprisingly fell into a deep sleep not stirring until the morning's fingers of light, crept into her room and trailed across her sleeping face.

As soon as Anna opened her eyes she was instantly alert and flinging the bedcovers back jumped out of bed, slipping into her slippers as she went, which meant hopping some of the way with one slipper on and the other nearly there! Immediately she went to the front window and looked out on to the little green. The only movement there was a lone rabbit grazing on the grass with complete indifference to anything going on around it. All was still and quiet at the moment and the door opposite firmly shut and in darkness.

Sandy came up behind her and also peered out of the window observing the same normal scene.

"Did we just imagine what we saw last night?"

Anna shrugged her shoulders and raised her eyebrows as if to say, "You know we didn't, we saw what we saw and it was not good!"

They both left the window and without a word started to prepare breakfast, both in their own little world and deep in contemplation.

After they had finished breakfast they both got dressed and discussed what they were going to do, taking into consideration the dismal looking weather and the fact that, for the time of year, it was quite cold. They decided to go for a stroll to the front and then would make up their minds what to do, if the weather brightened then they would go for a longer walk and explore their surroundings.

Half an hour later they were both ready and prepared for anything, rain, wind, cold, whatever the elements threw at them really! They looked so good with their boots, jeans, waterproofs and hoods that before they left for the great outdoors they took a selfie, which was not easy, and then bundled out of the door both laughing and chattering at the same time. You really would not expect this type of weather in June however, it was England and therefore anything was possible, they supposed. To the rendition of "Hi Ho" they made their way across the green and out towards the car park, on their way to the seafront.

They chatted easily on the way to the front and said good morning to a few intrepid holiday-makers who had also ventured out. Some they noticed even had shorts on and were carrying buckets and spades for the children. What did you do when you had two or three little ones and the weather was horrendous, well you just carried on regardless as the kids wouldn't notice so long as there was sand and water they would be happy. They negotiated the little tunnel under the railway line in single file and carried on towards the front. There were several fairly modern little shops that were dotted along the boardwalk and they drifted in and out looking at all the wares on offer, omitting to buy sunglasses, for obvious reasons! When they emerged from the last shop before the seafront Anna caught sight of the man from the previous evening. He was still wearing the same clothes and had his head down against the wind and drizzle. They both looked at each other and, as if by some unspoken signal, they began to follow him. He walked up to the railings before the beach and there he pulled out his mobile and began making a call, talking into it held against his hunched up shoulder to protect it from the wind. Once finished he furtively looked around him causing the two friends to assume a nonchalant stance, even getting out a map of the town to look at in order that they did not look too conspicuous.

"I feel like Miss Marple," whispered Sandy with a giggle, to which Anna replied, "Yes, so do I, cool isn't it but a little scary too."

"I bet he is just an ordinary bloke and not doing anything suspicious at all and is just having a break at the seaside, like us."

Sandy looked at her and raised one eyebrow as if to say "Really?"

Anna shook her head and continued to pretend to look at the map whilst watching the man over the top of the flapping paper. Suddenly he disappeared onto the sand and in unison they packed up the map and followed to the railings to see if they could spot him. Just then, Sandy had an alert on her phone 'breaking news' it said so she just had to have a peek to see what it was.

> **'Missing woman… last seen three days ago… could be in the Exeter area… name… Catherine Dubois. Worked as a PA to successful businessman Jake Bonham who police want to question'…**

Sandy and Anna looked at each other and then looked over the railings scanning the beach in both directions. Their mystery man was hunched down by an outcrop of rocks and had been digging furiously by the looks of things, as there was a mound of wet sand piled up to the side of him. He seemed to be lowering something into the hole and then began to scoop the sand back, smoothing the top and then pushing the sand in tightly with the heel of his shoe. He then caught hold of the top of his hat where it peaked in the front, drawing it down over his forehead and looked around. By this time, the girls had moved away from the edge of the railings and had their backs to him, both realising that he was going to make a move and did not want to be seen staring in his direction. Sandy ducked under her arm to observe him and he walked over to the steps about two hundred yards away from them, climbed to the top and made off up the little path to their right. It was blowing an absolute hooley and the girls started to follow him at a distance, nonchalantly stopping every now and then to look at the sea or point at the rocks, in order to look like ordinary visitors on a walk. They were so busy trying not to be seen that they did not realise exactly where they were heading and suddenly found themselves coming down a little gravel path onto a high wall that stretched what seemed like, miles into the distance. On one side of them was a sheer drop to the sandy beach and on the other a low wall, the other side of which was the railway line. Anna froze, this was an absolute nightmare for her as she suffered from panic attacks if she found herself in an awkward situation or, somewhere she felt trapped, and boy, did she feel trapped and out of her comfort zone.

Meanwhile Sandy was plodding on behind her still talking ten to the dozen with her coat pulled up around her, eyes streaming from the wind and asking where the heck were they, as she couldn't see a thing. Anna felt the panic rising up her whole body and did not think she could go on but when she looked back they had come such a long way and she did not think she could go back either.

It absolutely terrified her that a train would whoosh past them at any minute and it would be so close they could almost touch it! Luckily for them the tide was not in, as that would have been it and she would not have moved another inch. The visibility was really bad and she could see no end to this path, it just seemed to go on forever. Luckily she could still see the man ahead of them but he was travelling at quite a pace, despite his slight limp, and it probably would not be long before she lost sight of him. However did they get themselves into this situation and in her head she could imagine being rescued from 'The Wall' by the coastguards, as she did not think she could continue. All of a sudden she heard a sort of wail behind her and when she looked back, Sandy had slipped off the wall and was clutching the gravel path for grim death.

Not ever knowing how she had managed it, Anna retraced her steps until she was abreast of Sandy and caught hold of her hands. Sandy was flailing about quite a bit, so she shouted to her to keep still and try and get a purchase with her feet. The top half of Sandy was bent over the path and it was therefore easier to grab the back of her coat and to pull for all she was worth, inch by painful inch, helping her get back onto the top of the wall.

Sandy was pushing with her feet and scrabbling up the concrete, until eventually, and with a painful grunt, she landed on the path next to Anna. For a fair amount of time they both just lay there, where they were on the path, oblivious to the wind, rain or cold just catching their breath and wholeheartedly grateful for being in one piece, albeit totally shattered and now shivering with nerves and the cold that was starting to seep into their very beings. Anna got to her feet first and then hauled Sandy to hers. "Umph… said Sandy, her little body shaking with nerves and fright. I just don't know what happened, one minute I was tottering along after you and the next I was halfway down to the sandy beach below and that is a long way down." As she uttered the last words Sandy's body convulsed in a huge shiver which went from her head to her toes.

It was the thought of the what-if's that took its toll on her runaway mind. Just then they both heard a loud whirring noise that seemed to get closer and closer. They turned and put their backs against the low wall, Anna not caring if a train came by as she was totally consumed by what was in front of her at the moment. An almighty helicopter was heading straight for them and it was tipping slightly towards the path.

Sandy was frozen to the spot and just slid down the wall, to land with a bump at the bottom, her head down on her chest as if to ward off the noise and the rushing wind the helicopter was creating. Anna looked up and she could see a man with an orange jumpsuit on, headgear and mask, looking out of the open sliding door on the side of the copter. He held onto the top of the doorway and leaned slightly out and using a sort of small loud hailer shouted down to them.

"You alright down there ladies?" He was making a thumbs up sign with his hand and waiting for their response. Anna looked up against the rushing wind and felt the whirring of the blades travelling through her whole chest as if it was slicing through her. She cupped her hands around her mouth to try and amplify her voice, "Yes, we are ok now, thank you, she shouted, also putting up her thumb in the affirmative. We were in a bit of bother but have managed to recover."

"Will you be alright to walk along to the next town? No bones broken? If we were to try and winch you up it could be tricky being so close to the edge and the railway line."

As if on cue a high-speed train zipped by behind them nearly making Sandy throw up her breakfast.

Anna, by now, had gone beyond scared and was just totally numb.

"I think we can do it. How far is it?"

The young man consulted with his teammate and then shouted down, "About another fifteen minutes. You are over the worst as from now on you will start to get some shelter from those rocks coming up and then you will enter the town underneath the railway bridge."

Anna looked down at Sandy who was looking very pale and was obviously very cold and shaken up. The young man followed her gaze and nodded to himself as if making a decision.

"Stay where you are, we will send someone to come and help you. Ok?"

Anna nodded and put her thumb up again giving him a huge grin of relief which he understood.

The copter immediately backed off and dipped away from where they were. They saw it hover over the beach a way ahead, and a man was winched down onto the sand. He hit the ground running and scaled the wall to appear by their side within a few minutes. He quickly knelt down to Sandy who, by now, was looking a little better and after examining her, and checking the grazes she had sustained on her legs and ankles, helped her to her feet. Putting his arm around her he started off towards the rocks in the distance, Anna bringing up the rear.

She had to admit it felt a lot better now he had taken charge and was helping Sandy, talking quietly to her all the time. Anna had completely forgotten her panic and just focused on getting back in one piece! It did not take long to get to the end of the path and after going down a ramp to beach level, the seafront came into view. The young pilot, whose name was Andrew, asked if they wanted him to call an ambulance in order that they could be checked over but they refused. Sandy was now looking much better and her colour had returned. Making sure they were on the right way to the nearest coffee shop, Andrew took his leave of them with a quick salute.

"Thank you so much for coming to our rescue, you do an amazing job and we are so sorry if we kept you from a real emergency."

Andrew smiled broadly and said it was a pleasure to be of help to such lovely ladies and he did not think they had 'wasted his time', as it could have been a lot worse if they had not been patrolling the area. Anna was now very curious and she tapped him on the shoulder as he would have made to leave.

"Can you tell us if you were looking for someone in particular or is it just a regular exercise?"

Andrew turned and put his hands on his hips, "Oh, No, this is not a regular exercise, we are looking for a missing person."

The two friends looked at each other and their faces did not reflect what they were feeling or thinking.

"Thank you again Andrew, and we hope you find your missing person soon."

Andrew took his leave and returned to his helicopter making a circling motion with his hand in the air.

The helicopter's blades immediately began to rotate and with a quick wave in their direction, he ducked under the force of the blades and swung himself up inside the side door. Once he was fully on board the helicopter lifted off and very quickly disappeared along the coast.

What the two girls did not know, was the mystery man had stopped by an old brick tunnel, to smoke a cigarette and had been watching them for some time. As they moved off to enter the town he threw down his half-smoked butt and, pulling his hat down over his eyes, proceeded in the same direction to the town.

Luckily for Anna and Sandy there was a lovely little tea shop just across the road from the beach and they made their way rapidly towards it. The door had a little bell attached to it and they found a table by the window and gratefully sank onto the padded seats with a sigh. It was not long before, their order having been taken by the young waitress, a large pot of tea was put before them with milk, sugar and two large sultana scones, cream and jam. They had not spoken really since saying goodbye to Andrew, but it was by mutual consent and felt comfortable after their traumatic ordeal. Anna poured the steaming tea into the cups, adding the milk and spreading the clotted cream on her scone, with a large dollop of jam.

"Well, said Anna, you did say a mini adventure but I had no

idea it would be a full-blown, gigantic, humungous one, Sandy. My mind and body are still reeling from the trauma we have just experienced. How are you feeling now after your hot cup of tea my dear?"

Sandy had both hands firmly place around her cup and had been savouring the hot sweet tea, yes, she had sugared it even though normally she did not take it.

"Umm, I really don't know, I feel kind of strange, as if what just happened did not happen to us, it was like a nightmare from which you could not awake. My legs sting a little but they are not too bad. When I go to the loo in a minute I will wash and clean the small grazes, I have some antiseptic cream in my bag."

Anna looked concerned and said maybe they should go to A & E to get her checked out and also get a tetanus jab. Sandy assured her she was ok and her tetanus inoculations were up-to-date, ending that her pride had taken more of a battering than her body! When they had warmed up, eaten their scones and finished their tea Sandy cleaned her grazes and they went just across the road to the bus stop where they could catch a bus back to the chalet. Both women knew they would not attempt that perilous walk again!

The bus disgorged them at their stop and they made their way back to the chalet, not stopping for food this time as, by mutual consent, they had agreed to have scrambled eggs on toast that evening with a mug of chocolate to help them sleep. It had been a very full, dramatic and exhausting day by anyone's standards and they were pooped. They did not see the stranger enter his chalet just after they arrived, nor did they see him glance over to theirs with a much-determined look on his face. They had no idea of the danger they were in or what they had stumbled upon in this sleepy, old fashioned seaside town.

5:

Mysterious Stranger

The man let himself into his holiday let and once inside started to pace. He went to the kitchen and poured himself a glass of whiskey, which he downed in one! "Stupid women, he muttered to himself, meddling fools!" "What had they seen, if anything, and why were they following him as no women of their age would walk along that perilous path unless motivated by curiosity. Hopefully that is all it was, but if not, how would he deal with them?" This had turned into a complete nightmare and one that was running out of control. That stupid bitch of a PA he had an affair with, it was meant to be just a 'bit of fun' on the side. No harm done, they were both adults and she knew he was married and had no intention of leaving his wife. He had been totally naive to let her know so much about his dealings in the business and how he was creaming off large slices of the profits and siphoning it all into an offshore account. He thought he could 'pay her off' and being the addle-headed little nothing she was, she would keep quiet and be grateful for her windfall. Not so Catherine, she wanted more, she wanted a half share or she would blab. She had pushed him to his utmost limits, and he admitted to himself that he was a womaniser, a complete A-hole and, an outright thief but, was he capable of more than that? What did he do with her? Would it just take him offering her more money to evaporate from his life? This had been his dilemma until yesterday evening. Catherine had been baiting him at work all day and kept threatening to pick up her phone to call his wife, Eva. Each time she had put the phone down and just stared at him, grinning wickedly, then actually laughing like a bloody hyena. What had he seen in her? Had something addled his brain as, technically, she was not classically pretty but she was mildly attractive and, as he was being true to form, that was enough to reel him in! He was such a loser, such a mug, he bought into everything, the flattery, the adoration, and of course the sex, she was good at that, he had to concede. However, it was all a tangled web to deceive and trap him and he was the unsuspecting fly now neck-deep in the sticky stuff! Last night, he did not want to think about it or go over it in his mind as it was the stuff horror stories are made of, only this time it was real!

To add to his miseries, he now suspected the two older women in the holiday let opposite him, had a very unnatural interest in his daily life. Why else would they follow him along that dangerous pathway on such an evil day? No one in their right minds, except him, would take that path. The fact that they got into trouble and had to be rescued said it all but what did they know exactly?

He knew he was wanted by the police and had planned to go back to London and then phone them, saying he had been on a business trip and not heard the news as he had been ill. He had it all planned, as he was due to complete a deal tomorrow with a good client of his and was going to cancel the appointment due to illness. He had hotel receipts for the two previous days, having checked in early and then gone back to check out on the second day. The holiday let he had booked under a false name and had seen no-one on checking in, as it had all been done by email and online banking, and he had received an entry code by text on arrival. That bit, at least, had gone smoothly the rest was just a complete mess!

Added to all this he had recently undergone keyhole surgery on his knee and he was walking with a definite limp still, trying to take the weight off the injured knee. How had it all come to this? He had arranged to meet Catherine at the holiday let and he hoped she would drop her intention to expose him as he was going to offer her a lot more money, more than he could actually afford, but he would worry about that later, if it got her off his back. He had arrived at the let as arranged but, on entering, had discovered Catherine's Lifeless body sprawled on the floor of the little sitting-room. To say he was horrified with the discovery and that he had totally freaked out would be an understatement. What the hell had happened and what did he do now? This was a mess, a bloody mess. He lowered his head into his hands at that point and sobbed like a baby. He may be a lot of things but killer he was not, and the thought of it made him wretch and run for the bathroom where he was violently sick. He felt panic welling up in his stomach and his mind went totally blank. Did he ring the police? If he did they would investigate everything and the whole sordid affair would be exposed. They would accuse him of the murder, lock him up and throw away the key. He had gathered from the position Catherine's body was lying and the pool of blood coming from her temple that it had been a heavy blow to her head.

Jake had pulled his leather gloves from the pocket of his coat and twisted his hands into them, shaking so much it was no easy task. He had to see if she was, indeed dead as that would change everything. Taking deep breaths, he had approached her body and, pulling a pocket knife out of his suit jacket he exposed the shiny blade. Trying not to actually look at her, he held the blade in front of her nose and mouth. If she was still breathing there would be moisture on the cold blade. Part of him hoped he was wrong but on inspection, the blade was clean. He called her name and shook her but there was absolutely no response. Oh my God! Shit! This was unreal what the hell did he do now. His knee was killing him and he stood up away from her body. The shaking started again and he began to pace, his thought process worked better that way.

He should come clean and to hell with the consequences, he did not do it and a really good lawyer could prove it. Just then his mobile phone rang which made him jump, set his heart racing and pumping the blood around his body at a million miles an hour. He sat down on the hard chair and pulled out his phone. It was his wife! What a bloody wonderful time to call, but then, that was Eva all over, wasn't it?

Eva the Diva he had nicknamed her as she was spoilt beyond belief first, by her father and then by him, pathetic bastard that he was. Her father had all the money and held all the cards. He had to give Eva what she wanted or Daddy would tighten the purse strings and kick him out of his job. He had been trying to secure some money from the business in order to wean himself off the two of them, sucking him dry of all the emotional and ambitious juices he once possessed. It was the reason he had affairs, as Eva was like a black widow spider, weaving her poisonous web around him, and it afforded him time out, away from her venomous nest. He had pushed his gloved fingers through his damp, limp hair and pushed the green button. What he encountered on the other end of the phone totally shook him to the core. Eva was screaming down the phone, crying and wailing and making no coherent sense.

"I didn't mean it, I just meant to warn her off, like all the other mindless prostitutes who have thrown themselves at you. I have known about your affair for weeks, the pattern is always the same and you are always over-generous to me, whilst suddenly going on loads of business meetings with overnight stays. I found out you had booked the holiday chalet by checking your phone when you had a shower, you never cover your tracks, it is too easy. I then changed the time she was to meet you and got here before she arrived. As you can imagine she was totally unprepared to find me there and not best pleased. I told her a few home truths about your string of affairs and how you always come back to me in the end. I was not prepared for her lack of control and immediate physical onslaught. She came at me like a banshee flailing her arms and grabbing my hair. I just don't remember what actually happened next but I must have shoved her hard, to get her away from me, and she stumbled backwards, hitting her head on the stone mantel over the small fireplace. She did not even scream, there was just a sickening thud and she landed awkwardly on the floor, blood seeping from her head. She didn't move, Christ, she was so still. I just totally lost it and began screaming at her to get up, stupid trollop, just get up! Nothing, no sound, no movement just the sticky, red mass oozing from the gash in her head and seeping into the pale rug." Eva took in a laboured breath and then went on…

"I should have called an ambulance then, although I knew it was too late, but I was frozen, body and mind. I looked out of the window and the place was deserted, there were not many occupied chalets as it was early in the season and the weather was dismal. I just opened the front door and left quietly, walking quickly along the path to my car. I encountered no one on the way and once in my car I just sat there, head in hands, sobbing and rocking myself backwards and forwards appalled at what had happened. Like a mantra, I could hear myself saying over and over, what have I done, what have I done? Eventually I pulled myself together enough to start the car and move out of the car park and how, I have no idea, got home."

With that last statement Eva made an agonised sound like a wounded animal and sobbed quietly into the phone. Then as if realising she was still holding the mobile she whispered, "You are there now, I know you are? What are you going to do, what the hell are you going to do Jake?"

There was a long silence as Jake tried to take in all the information Eva had just given him and process it.

Eva was an outright cow, shallow, selfish and needy but not a killer, or so he thought but this mess was, in part, his doing too, as he knew his affairs were an accepted part of their bizarre marriage as Eva knew he had to stray in order to keep him, it was in his DNA. During the time of his affairs were the best moments of his marriage. He needed that edge, the excitement and subterfuge and, in her own way, so did Eva as each time he strayed their 'make-up' sex was fantastic. Jake hunched his shoulders forward and put one hand over his eyes then, spanning his face with forefinger and thumb, squeezed his temples as if to eradicate the scene before him.

"Jake!" came Eva's sharp cry, what are you going to do?"

"What I always do, Eva, give in to you and clear up this almighty, gruesome, mess which, at this precise moment in time, I have no idea how, but will ring you after I have figured it out."

Jake cut her off, as he could stand her whimpering and sobbing no more, it was not in character and made her weak and vulnerable which she was normally neither. He had to get rid of Catherine's body and quickly. She was lying on the big rug before the fireplace so he would wrap her up in that. It was a start.

Before long Jake had wrapped the body in the rug and then using several black bin liners had inched them over the roll securing them all along with twine he had found in a drawer. Thankfully they were not flimsy liners but quite thick strong ones and would not rip that easily. It made it so much easier not seeing her as he worked but he still felt nauseous and clammy, stopping several times to gather himself. As he was composing himself by taking several deep breaths, his eyes closed and his head slumped down on his chest, he suddenly became aware of something glinting on the carpet, which must have fallen from the rug as he moved it. Jake scooped it up and on examination realised it was Eva's locket, a gift from daddy, which she treasured. Bollocks, he would have to try and get rid of it, he began to shake again, an all-over trembling of frustration, anger and fear. One more bloody complication for him to have to sort out for her but, sort it out he must, just not now as he had a more pressing job to do, getting rid of the body, before he could turn his attention to the locket.

Focusing his mind to the task in hand, he realised, he would have to drag her body to the car and find somewhere to hide it, hopefully for good! He did not dare think about what he was doing or he would be lost he just worked on autopilot. By now it was very late evening and all was quiet in the park. The weather was foul with wind and rain, so just right for what he had to do. On his phone he searched on Google Earth for any old quarries in the area or any likely places he could hide the body. Bingo, there was an old disused clay quarry about half an hour away and scouting round it looked ideal with an abandoned slurry pool at the bottom.

Jake checked outside for any movement, but as it was 2 o'clock in the morning, as he expected, all was still and quiet.

He had pulled Catherine's body to the front door and now had to get it out and to the car. Unfortunately the front door made quite a loud noise when he opened it and he stopped, checking outside as before. All was still quiet, so he hauled the heavy parcel out of the door and on to the path. He then closed the door as quietly as he could and began to drag her body along the path. At first there was some scraping along the gravel but once onto the concrete, where he had fastened two little pulleys on to it, it moved fairly smoothly. Getting it to the car was something else and he tried to keep in the shadows as much as possible in case of cameras. He had fortunately parked the car on the nearside edge of the car park and although it took great effort and his knee gave him hell, he got the body in the boot and closed and locked it. By now he was sweating profusely and he was experiencing acute pain in his knee, which also made him want to throw up. He backed the car out of the car park and set the sat nav for his destination. It was an absolutely foul night and the windscreen wipers could not cope with the amount of water being thrown at them, making visibility almost non-existent. Damn, he should have gone to Specsavers, was the totally inappropriate thought that entered his head and it was not even remotely funny, but it was relevant, as he had been having trouble with his vision for some months now and had put off going to the opticians; because he was a man and men did not need glasses, ok! However, he wished he had because he was crawling along and the road was totally awash with water, great lakes forming at the side of the road. At this precise moment in time he also wished he had the four by four instead of his snazzy sports car. Shit! He had missed the turning and nearly smashed into a huge wall that had loomed up in front of him. He sat there for a while, panting, although he had not been running, the sweat pouring from his temple. He found a tissue and wiped his forehead and hands, which were shaking like a geriatric. Hell, what had he got himself into for that idiotic, leech of a psycho woman.

He tried to think of more expletives but none would adequately describe how he felt right now. His lights picked out a gravel track leading downwards but, how good it was, or how safe he had no idea as it was pitch black all around. He had a powerful torch in the back which he twisted around to retrieve. He switched it on and thankfully it did have a really powerful beam which he hoped would help him somewhat. Pulling on his hat and hunching up in his waterproof he opened the door, which was nearly pulled away from his hand by the force of the wind outside. He really did not want to do this, it was utter madness, what he wanted was to be back at home with a stiff glass of whiskey in his hand and the warmth of the central heating seeping through his cold body. Well, in reality he was not there and he had no bloody choice. He got out of the car and shone the torch beyond the headlights. The road, if you could call it that, was not as steep as he had first thought and was bordered on one side by a low wall. He scrambled back to the car and edged it forward, very cautiously, his foot hovering over the brake, as he inched forwards as slowly as he could.

He gradually emerged at the bottom where the ground was fairly flat and saw before him, illuminated in the headlights, what looked like an expanse of muddy water. He assessed the situation and found that he could position the car next to the water, which would make submerging the body a little easier. He got out of the car, carrying the torch, which he put on the ground giving him a little light by which to operate. He opened the boot and began to heave out the parcel, which now seemed much heavier than when he put it in! It took a while but, eventually he managed to pivot it so that it landed with a thud on the stony ground. He felt sick again, and bent over trying to suck in some much-needed air and alleviate the nausea. He knew he would have to weight down the body or it would not sink, so he looked around for some large rocks. Fortunately, due to the nature of the area they were scattered all around and he chose several fairly large ones.

Managing to open the outside sack, he started to stuff the rocks inside, spacing them out fairly evenly and then he secured the sack again with some tougher rope he had brought with him for the job. Once this had been done, he pushed and heaved the huge black bundle towards the muddy lake. Eventually he pushed it far enough over the side for it to be top-heavy and, with the added weight of the rocks, it took on a life of its own and began to slither forward into the muddy blackness beneath.

Slowly, inch by painful inch it disappeared into the water suddenly upending and eerily rising up and then was completely swallowed in one fluid movement, with just a few wayward bubbles to show its entry into the water.

Jake turned the light, he had retrieved from the ground, onto the water and he could see nothing but some ripples on the surface, which gently formed a circle and then was gone. He did not know he had been holding his breath and he just heaved a great sigh of relief that the job was done. He was completely soaked, his hair plastered to his head and even his waterproof was totally sodden. Looking down at his feet he could see the clay spattered all over them and knew that they had to be discarded along with everything else he was wearing. He had brought some more plastic bags with him which he laid over the seats and the floor to minimise the mess when he got in. Now to get back, have a boiling hot shower, dispose of the clothing and get some sleep. He would explain the rug to the owners, saying he had ruined it, and they could bill him for it. It would be hard to sleep there tonight but he had to make sure he cleaned everything up and left nothing incriminating behind.

6:
Curiosity Killed the Cat

Anna and Sandy awoke to the sound of birds singing and warm sun streaming through their windows. Anna was totally overwhelmed by the patch of blue sky she could see from her little window, as the weather had been so awful during their stay, that she actually believed someone had stolen the sun for the summer! They both pottered around, making tea and preparing breakfast, Anna even breaking out into song, which, to be fair, she normally did most mornings to the disgust of her long-suffering other half. She had been a vocalist for many years with a big band and had always regretted having to give it up. Good memories of a golden era now long gone. Sandy, on the other hand loved to hear her warble, as she lived on her own now, her dear husband having passed many years ago, so she enjoyed hearing her friend bustling about and humming her favourite oldies. At that precise moment Anna pretended a spoon was the microphone and announced breakfast was about to be served in the formal dining room! Sandy had to chuckle, as she knew her friend was totally bonkers, always had been, but she loved it as you never quite knew what she would do next, creating a little drama out of everyday mundane tasks.

"On the menu today, we have deliciously crunchy, rock hard, pretty much inedible burnt toast. Ta Dah!" said Anna with a huge flourish putting the offerings on the table with jam and golden syrup.

Sandy laughed out loud with her pretty face wreathed in

smiles and took a seat at the breakfast table to begin her first meal of the day. They even had boiled eggs this morning, so began to tap them with their spoons before dunking the 'not burnt' golden toast. They munched away for a while before Anna looked at Sandy and the outspoken question about yesterday was voiced.

"How did we get ourselves into that terrifying ordeal yesterday, following that stupid man with his silly limp along that dangerous pathway? I don't even remember how we got there really as, one minute we were at the seafront, and the next we were being rescued from a really dangerous situation."

Sandy nodded sagely whilst stuffing a piece of toast in her mouth.

"I don't know either but I do know I shall never attempt that journey again, I thought I was a goner when I slipped over the edge, and want to thank you again for hauling me up, the rest is just a blur really."

Anna agreed as she had never been so terrified in her life and really still did not know how she managed to drag her friend up and complete the journey without passing out.

"That mysterious man was shifty though and why did he go along that perilous path, also did he bury something by the rocks?"

The girls looked at each other then, as if just remembering what they had seen yesterday and what it could mean. "I suppose he could have been doing anything really," said Sandy, shrugging her shoulders. Although, what would you want to bury by some rocks on a seafront?"

They lapsed into silence and then stared at each other across the little kitchen table, both deep in thought, and more than a little spooked by what had happened.

They decided they would go to the seafront after they had cleared the breakfast things away, and let the strong wind blow away the cobwebs, so they could think more clearly. They let themselves out of the chalet and the weather was much better and warmer today although coats were still needed as it was blustery. They made their way around the little grassy courtyard not seeing anyone this morning and began to take the path leading to the Reception building. Suddenly, Anna felt a hand on her shoulder, which made her squeak, and she actually jumped on the spot. She heard Sandy's quick intake of breath and, as she turned around, their mystery man was standing behind them. He was smiling and looked pleasant enough this morning, although there was still a hard set to his jawline and a muscle was twitching by his mouth.

"Good morning, ladies, and what a fine one it is for a change. I see you are off for an outing, not as dangerous as yesterday I hope?" This said with a twist to his mouth and an arch to his eyebrow!

Ah hah! thought Anna, he did see us yesterday and knows we were following him, this was not looking good. Anna, looked up at him and smiled broadly, shaking her head from side to side.

"Oh, No! We have learnt our lesson not to venture too far and get ourselves into danger, we only meant to see if we could get to the next town along the front, not realising it was so narrow and slippery due to the awful weather. We feel rather silly for causing such a fuss."

"How did you know we got into bother?"

The man stepped back a little and surveyed them both, charm oozing from him.

"Oh, I was taking five, having a smoke, away from the wind and rain, under the old brick tunnel, which leads to the entrance to Dawlish Warren. I saw the helicopter touch down, so, intrigued, I stayed there and saw them rescue you both and check you over. I do hope you are no worse for wear today after your ordeal?"

This said with a very tight-lipped smile and an edge to his silky deep voice.

"No, said Sandy, far from it, we feel fine, just glad it was no worse. We go home soon, so will play it very safe from now on, no more rock climbing for us!" Sandy said this with a little break to her voice, as by now she was getting very agitated and felt this man was quizzing them in order to see if they had followed him deliberately or, if they truly were two silly females on holiday with no sense of direction! Anna gave a rather forced laugh and caught hold of Sandy's hand pulling her on down the path.

"Sorry, we can't stop, as we have to catch a bus and there is not another one for ages, nice meeting you."

With that she pulled Sandy behind her nearly making her lose her balance, before they both scuttled over the car park and up to the main road. They were both flustered and out of breath by the time they got to the front and kept looking behind them, to see if he had followed them. As luck would have it, the bus to Dawlish Warren was waiting at the stop, so they scrambled on board needing to get away from the horrible man. If he had been following them then he would have seen they had caught a bus and hopefully would then leave them alone.

They flopped into the bucket seats, after paying their fares to the driver, and just sat for a time getting their breath back and calming down. Sandy was the first to break the silence and said, "Do you think he suspects us Anna? He seemed very interested as to why we were on the path. I didn't like him one bit for all his charm, he had an edge to him and a steely hard stare, it really sent shivers down my spine." Anna was deep in thought and nodded her agreement. "Trouble is, he has made us more suspicious than ever and I for one, think he has been up to no good, I wonder what he was doing under that tunnel?" Both friends looked at each other and Sandy replied, "I don't know, but I think whilst we are here we should check that out."

When they got to the town they found their little cafe and had a strong cup of tea, to calm their nerves and a toasted sandwich, then once fed and watered they made their way to the seafront to where they quickly identified the old brick tunnel he was sheltering under. It was definitely a better day today and was very pleasant walking along the sand. When they got to the tunnel, they had a look round, it was fairly gloomy under there but they could make out the walls and the uneven floor. They walked around a little more, to let their eyes adjust to the gloom and Anna saw a flattened cigarette butt on the ground. Suddenly, looking up, Sandy saw something pale against the rocks and reached up to try and see what it was. A tiny piece of material was poking out of a crevice just above her head. Going on tiptoe, she tried to see if the grey stone would budge and, sure enough, as she pulled and wiggled it, it eventually fell out. Reaching into the hole it made, she grasped a muslin type piece of material and pulled. It was a cloth bag filled with something. Anna came to help and they made sure no one was around and checked the path both ways. They opened the bag and felt inside pulling out first a purse, some keys on a key ring and a mobile phone. The keyring was quite distinctive with a designer logo made of little crystals and attached were several different sets of keys. The mobile was a very expensive, top of the range model, and had the initials CD written in gold lettering on the front of the case. Both women looked at each other and silently mouthed the initials, the missing woman the police were looking for was Catherine Dubois, C D, this was no small coincidence, it was a huge one! Anna made a quick decision and started to stuff the articles back into the bag. Sandy realised what she was going to do and picked up the stone with which to seal the hole up again. Anna broke the awful silence first saying, "We have to notify the police but we cannot take the chance of moving this evidence in case he comes back and finds the bag missing, puts two and two together after our meeting and comes after us."

Once they had finished putting the stone back, making sure all looked as before, they turned to retrace their steps back to the beach to catch a bus back to Dawlish. They were both shaking from head to foot by the time they reached the town and sat down on a bench in the little square. They kept looking around them expecting to be pounced on at any minute. Sandy looked at the bus timetable and worked out it would be another twenty minutes until they could catch their bus. They popped in the little cake shop and purchased a bottle of water and a couple of iced buns.

It would keep the wolf from the door for now. By the time they had finished their food the bus arrived and they were on their way back. They had to notify the police about what they had found and their suspicions about the mystery man, but they could not risk the police coming to their chalet, they would have to meet them somewhere in the town. They hurried off the bus and started to walk back to their chalet, stopping at the little supermarket for some ham and salad for their evening meal. They still had plenty of tea, coffee and milk so it did not take them long to complete their purchases. Once finished at the supermarket they each carried a bag and started to walk briskly back to their little 'home' as they now knew it. It was still not busy and there were very few people about, the little parade of shops was empty. They let themselves in but, as Sandy went to close the door, it was shoved from the other side, actually causing her to fall backwards, tripping over a chair by the table. Anna recovered first and went to help her friend up from the floor as, behind her, stood their Mystery man and he was not smiling now!

When he had forced his way in, he had slammed the door shut behind him with the heel of his foot, and he seemed twice as tall as this morning, with a menacing air about him.

"What the hell are you doing, barging into our home and knocking us flying, you moron?" shouted Anna. "As if we have not had enough to contend with on this holiday, without you making it worse."

"State your business and clear off we have nothing that you want, no money or valuables, so go rob someone else."

The man began to smile but not in a nice way, it was more of a sneer.

"My, you are a feisty one, I'll grant you that but methinks you are in no position to give me an ultimatum. I think you two nosy parker's have got yourself into a lot of trouble and you had both better sit down and listen."

Anna helped Sandy to the couch and after checking she was ok, sat down next to her, close enough to feel how badly she was shaking. Anna reached for her hand and squeezed it tightly before facing the man squarely. "What is this all about, we are just two friends having a few days holiday together, why should that upset you so much?"

The man pulled out a chair from the table and, pulling it round so the seat faced him, he straddled it, putting his arms across the back to stare at them.

"What do you think you have seen and where did you go to today? I really do not have the time to spend out of my busy schedule trying to second guess two idiotic, bored, postmenopausal women acting strangely.

I know you have been spying on me, and why you followed me along that perilous shoreside path I have no idea. So ladies, spill, who is going to tell me what you have been up to and has it spiced up your seaside jolly?"

With that last remark he laughed out loud and slapped his knee (luckily for him his good knee!) hugely enjoying his own joke at their expense. Anna looked him squarely in the face, not flinching one little bit and delivered her scathing reply to his question. "We are enjoying a well-earned few days away catching up with each other's lives and families as we have not seen each other for a while, we certainly have no interest in a nasty, small-minded, bully like you. I think the boot is on the other foot and it is you who have the problem, one of paranoia and a persecution complex! We have no idea what you are talking about, and just want to catch the train home, as planned, tomorrow and would say to you that you must lead a very dull life to want to threaten two vulnerable women who have no interest in you, or your affairs, whatsoever."

Anna did not look away from him, holding his gaze the whole time she was talking, and he did have the grace to move back a little, as Anna was quite fired up by now and would not stand to be intimidated by this stranger. Jake slowly unfolded his long legs from the chair and stood up, looking at them both from his height advantage.

"I get your message loud and clear, but now you get mine, go back home tomorrow and stop meddling in things you do not understand, I have very important clients in this area and some crucial business meetings coming up, which I do not want sabotaged by two female idiots trying to spice up their vacation. DO YOU BOTH UNDERSTAND?"

Sandy pulled at Anna's Jacket and just nodded to her, then foolishly, looking at the man with frightened eyes, blurted out, "You have made your point and we will leave for Salisbury, as planned tomorrow, we do not want to be anywhere near you and have no intention of disrupting your business affairs, just learn some manners and make no mistake that we have absolutely no interest in your business whatsoever."

He scrutinised them both for what seemed like an age and then turned on his heel and left, just like that, he was gone, the door firmly slammed behind him.

There was utter silence after he had gone, the only detectable sound being the two friends gasping for air as the fright of what had just occurred took hold. They just sat there huddled together on the little sofa, Sandy was crying softly and shaking whilst Anna was trying to work out what to do next. This was for real and it was happening to them and they knew now that something bad had definitely happened here. The trouble was Anna felt they could not now contact the police here, they had to go home.

He would be watching their every move and if, for some reason, the police did not believe them, he would come back and that did not bear thinking about. She turned to Sandy and hugged her dear friend, then holding her at arms' length said, "We have to go home tomorrow, as we cannot report this here, he will be watching our every move, do you agree?"

Her friend just nodded and sniffed loudly, looking around for a tissue which she found in her pocket, to wipe her eyes and blow her nose.

"Yes, I agree, we have to act normally now and everything is booked for tomorrow, so we will have to wait until we get home to contact the police. We cannot take the risk of anything going wrong as he will be back! I have never been so afraid in all my life, I thought my heart would break out of my chest it was beating so loudly. Put the kettle on Anna as I think we need a cup of tea to calm our shattered nerves and it is the one normal thing we can do today!"

Anna gently smiled at her friend and went to do as she asked thinking that a stiff brandy would probably be more appropriate but they didn't have any and it would make them choke anyway! She bustled about filling the kettle and dropping tea bags into mugs. Once she had made the tea, she carried their two mugs over to the table and found some chocolate biscuits in the cupboard for extra sweetness to pep them both up. Sandy sat down opposite Anna at the table and sipped her hot tea with much appreciation finding it very calming. They both ate a biscuit and found they felt profoundly better after a little while. They agreed to pack their cases then have their meal, by which time it would be time for bed and hopefully they would feel more positive in the morning.

Jake had slammed the door of their chalet and thundered back to his, also slamming the door after his entry. He was fuming but also not sure what to do now. He had gone to see them on impulse and thought now that he should probably not have shown his hand. On reflection he did not think they knew anything and were just trying to relieve the boredom of a washed-out holiday. He raked his hand through his hair as though it would clear his thoughts but of course, as usual, it did not. Just then his phone started to vibrate on the coffee table and it lit up with a callers name. Jake leant over and saw it was from Eva, his wife! Oh No! he did not want to talk to her now he was too angry and frustrated. What the hell had he done, she was a witch, a clinging, screeching, demanding she-devil. The phone was vibrating madly sending it scooting over the polished table, clattering and flashing Eva's name as though she could see him sitting there debating whether to answer it or throw it across the room! Eventually he could stand it no longer and he swiped the phone from the table and punched the green flashing phone button. Immediately he heard her high-pitched frenzied voice coming from the phone. So startled was he by the ferocity of her tirade, that he almost did drop the phone.

"Are you there Jake or are you hiding under some grubby stone like the Lilly livered coward you are? Answer me, damn it, I demand you tell me what is happening, it is driving me crazy not knowing what you are doing and when you will come home. I ask you to do one thing for me and you drag your heels and bleat. I did not know she would go absolutely mental and I had to defend myself, it was an accident, a stupid accident for which I am not to blame."

Eva realised she was getting no response from the other end

of the phone and Jake could hear her sharp intake of breath, as if trying to compose herself, and then her tone changed to one of sickly sweet.

"Jake, my darling, I am sorry for getting so angry but it is pure hell here not knowing what is going on. I promise I have calmed down now and will listen to what you have to say, just talk to me, please?"

Jake was holding the phone in his hand and just staring at it whilst massaging his neck with his other hand, as if he could knead away this huge mistake he was sure he had made.

"I am here Eva, just! This is all a bloody mess and is getting more complicated every second."

There was silence on the other end of the phone and then he heard Eva take a huge breath, which told him she was only just keeping it together and not spitting pure venom down the phone in the hope it would shrivel him up and reduce him to a dry, cracked carcass.

"Look, lover, you have done what I asked you to do, you should be cleaning up the chalet and getting ready to leave, what is so complicated about that?"

Eva could not see him but Jake moved his eyes skywards and wondered if this woman even lived on the same planet as him.

"Eva, this has not been easy and I have been followed by two older women from bloody Salisbury, who are staying in the chalet opposite. I don't think they know anything and are just trying to spice up a boring holiday by latching on to me. I have read them the riot act and probably frightened the living daylights out of them, so I don't expect to be bothered further, although the blonde bitch is quite feisty. It is just an added complication I could have done without and hope they get on their ruddy train tomorrow, and just bugger off."

"Who the hell are they? What bloody chalet opposite? What do they think they have seen? This certainly complicates everything, what if you haven't scared them off? What if they stir things up by blabbing to someone? Oh Holy Shit, Jake, you have got to do something."

Jake had switched off the minute Eva had started her tirade of abuse, he was used to it by now. Eva could scorch the skin off a rhino with her acid tongue and she was in full lava flow right now.

The poor cows opposite did not know what they had got themselves into and he hoped they just went home tomorrow as he knew Eva would not let this go.

"Enough!" Jake shouted down the phone.

"I will sort it, Eva, just give it a rest. I will sort it like I always do for you and dear Daddy!"

"Don't you dare patronise me Jake, I mean it, you have got to make sure they do nothing or I will make sure they never damn well stick their beaks into anything ever again! Do you hear me? This is not an idle threat Jake, we are walking on a tightrope here and they could make sure we fall into the abyss. Any stupid, clumsy mistake at this stage could cause us to crash and burn, not me Jake, US!

Make no mistake that I will drag you down into the mire with me and force your head under it with my dainty, stiletto clad foot! ARE YOU LISTENING TO ME? J – A – K - E?"

"Christ Almighty Eva, if you go on like this, the whole bloody holiday park will know. I will deal with it. I have to think away from your screeching and wailing, woman. These two women are innocuous, they will go back to their little houses in Salisbury tomorrow and go back to their dull little lives again. I will call you tomorrow. Wait for my call but DO NOT do anything or go anywhere, DO YOU UNDERSTAND?"

He could hear Eva sobbing loudly and snivelling, her anger now evaporated temporarily, whilst she felt sorry for herself, having run out of suitable expletives to hurl at him Meekly she agreed and ended the call abruptly, leaving Jake staring at his phone in exasperation and molten anger.

She was an absolute nightmare with her volatile mood swings and control-freak nature. Why he had stood for it all this time he would never know, well yes, he did know, it was because of his position, power and money. He was so weak when it came to giving up the good life and when she was in a good 'phase' Eva was devastatingly fabulous to be with.

Jake sat there, hunched forwards in the chair, the heel of his hands on his forehead, which was damp with sweat, his mind in complete turmoil.

He poured himself a stiff whiskey and knocked it back in one, replenishing the glass almost immediately. Boy he needed that slug, it coursed through him like quicksilver, hitting his stomach with a warm punch. He sipped the second glass and ran his thumb around the rim.

He was sure the two women would scuttle off tomorrow as they planned and he would follow them, making sure they boarded the train, he would then return to London and get in touch with the police, saying he had just heard they wanted to question him and he would co-operate with their investigations. He had his alibi, he was a very busy man and most days had multiple meetings and appointments taking him all over the country and abroad. He had covered his tracks well and had used a false name to book into this holiday park and would pay in cash when he left.

After he had finished the second glass of spirit things looked a lot rosier and he had calmed down. He would deal with Eva later and when things blew over a little, would take her for a holiday on her private yacht moored in Italy. He could feel the sun beating down on his face and the salt of the spray as she powered through the water. Eva would adore that and things would be good between them again, at least for a while. He leant back in the chair and stretched out his long legs in front of him, allowing his whole body to relax for the first time in days. Not surprisingly he promptly fell into a deep sleep, which he would regret, not finding his bed, in the morning.

Eva punched the red phone symbol to end her call with Jake and realised she was shaking from head to foot. Not from nerves but pure, white-hot rage that frequently overtook her if she could not get her own way or a situation was spiralling out of control. Eva was a beautiful woman with a perfect figure and flawless skin but her beauty was marred by greed, lust, envy and above all her need for ultimate power and control. When she was little her father had indulged her frequent tantrums, not listening to her poor mother who tried to curb her daughter's growing problem. In the end she could not take any more, knowing there was something very wrong with her and facing verbal and physical abuse, on a daily basis. Her husband would not listen and accused her of not caring for Eva and being a disruptive influence In their marriage and had divorced her when Eva was 6 years old. Stephanie, Eva's mother, had never recovered from his rejection and had started to drink heavily after the divorce. Several years of alcohol abuse had finally taken its toll and she had passed away after a particularly heavy drinking binge, where she collapsed in her flat and was not discovered until it was too late.

Eva had become worse after her mother left and should have had medical help but her Father would not acknowledge that anything was wrong with his beautiful daughter. There had been incidences all through her school years but her Father had always managed to smooth them over. His money, position and influence always defused the situation and kept things out of the press.

Only one incident he could not entirely smother, was when Eva was at University and her boyfriend died of an overdose. He knew Eva had been acting strangely for months and had been more volatile than usual. Her doctor prescribed some antidepressants and sleeping pills, the same make as found in the boy's flat! As usual he had pulled strings and thrown money at the situation and Eva had not been implicated although, in his heart he knew she was in some way connected to his demise. It was very expertly covered up and not spoken of again.

For a while Eva had kept on an even keel and the medication helped. However, she met and married a businessman called Patrick O'Mara, a really nice guy and very successful. Everything was fine for about a year and then, unbeknown to anyone, Eva had stopped taking her meds and the arguments and tantrums had started. Patrick had not witnessed anything like it and had tried to placate her by indulging her every whim. This was never enough for Eva and she just spiralled out of control. It all culminated in a blazing, alcohol-induced row on their sleek yacht moored in Italy. The official verdict was that Patrick had been so drunk he had fallen over the side of the yacht, into the water, in the middle of the night, and drowned.

Again daddy came to her aid and it all went away.

Fast forward to the present and history was repeating itself again. Eva met and married Jake Bonham a talented businessman, but not wealthy by Eva's standards. Her father made him a director of the company and apart from Eva's demanding nature and high maintenance, their marriage had functioned well, if very one-sided, in favour of Eva's whims and temper.

That was until Jake's affairs! Most were just passing fancies and as soon as Eva found out he would drop them and their make-up sex would be fantastic.

Eva was in a white-hot fury and just wanted to get hold of these nosy women and neutralise them so that they did not bother her again. In her warped mind it was that easy and if she did not like something or someone then they were just wiped from her life as if they never existed.

Getting up from the chair Eva paced up and down, getting more and more agitated. What was it Jake said? Two older women, one blond, they were from Salisbury and, what was it? She tapped her head with her scarlet nails trying to remember. Yes! Yes! They were getting the train to Salisbury. Now she knew what she had to do.

Eva then made up her mind that she would go to Salisbury train station tomorrow and lay in wait for these two bitches, she knew they were older and was sure she could spot them, as they would be the ones faffing about and getting the porters to help them with their luggage. She would check the trains and see when the one from Dawlish was due into Salisbury. They would regret their stupid meddling into her affairs she would see to that!

7:

Boom!

The next morning Sandy and Anna had their breakfast as usual but were both very tired as neither had slept a wink all night. They had agreed that they would go back home and do some research on their mystery man. Before they left to catch the train today they would go to the office and see if they could find out if his name was the one they mentioned on the news, the day they were rescued. They knew the chalet he was in and there was an area in Reception where you could leave messages or, they would leave information for you. There were little pigeon holes in the wall marked with the chalet numbers with a little key hook at the bottom. When you vacated your holiday chalet you could leave it there if there was no-one on Reception. Hopefully there would be something, anything, that would give them a lead in finding his identity.

They packed their suitcases and discarded anything they did not need. There were instructions on how to dispose of their rubbish in the big bins outside the leisure complex. It must be said, that they were both feeling apprehensive, which was such a shame, as it was such a pretty little bungalow and they had enjoyed their short time away up until yesterday.

The weather was a little better and slightly warmer, so they dressed accordingly and got themselves ready to depart. Sandy did not have quite so much to take on the way back, thank goodness, and Anna had managed to condense hers to one suitcase. They did a final look around and made sure everything was tidy and clean and they had not left anything in the cupboards or drawers. They gave each other a comfort hug, both let out a sigh, then opened the front door ready to depart. The taxi had been booked for 12.30pm and they had used another company, fearing they could get stuck with the moron who had collected them! That meant that they had a good half an hour to go to Reception, hook up their key and look to see if there was anything in his pigeon hole, before waiting for the taxi to arrive. The train was due to leave at 1.20pm so that should give them plenty of time to have a snack and a coffee before boarding the train home. They had allowed for delays and thought they would get to Salisbury Station about four-ish and hopefully once there they would be able to grab a taxi for home.

Anna was staying with Sandy that night before being collected by her husband the following afternoon.

They made their way across the little green and down the path to the car park and Reception.

All the way there they were looking around them, worried that the man would pounce on them and threaten them again. By the time they reached the main building they were hot and bothered and both were shaking with nerves. When they entered the front office there was only one young girl on the desk and she was busy on the phone. They left their bags and walked slowly towards the post area.

Anna reached up and put their key on the hook whilst looking for the number of his chalet. It was just above theirs and she went on tiptoe to see if she could see anything wedged in there. As luck would have it she could see several sheets of folded paper, which she carefully withdrew. Turning away from the girl on the phone, she quickly rifled through them and thinking that she would not be lucky as most were just flyers advising of places to visit whilst on holiday, the last one contained some information regarding the cleaning of his chalet and had his name on the top, Mr Jack Brendon, not a million miles away from the real name and the same initials, which figured, as the moronic man did not seem too bright! Absolutely fabulous, this definitely tied it all in and proved they were on the right track and that he had been staying in the chalet opposite. Stuffing the papers back in the cubbyhole she walked over to Sandy as nonchalantly as she could and, facing her, inclined her head towards the door with a smile and a wink. Sandy got the message and they both made towards the exit.

"Hello, ladies, did you want me at all?" said the young girl behind the desk.

They both jumped a mile and turned simultaneously, even starting to speak together totally startled.

"Um, yes, we are fine thank you, we have just left our key on the hook, as requested in your itinerary."

"Oh, yes," said Anna quickly.

"Everything was paid for online so hopefully you do not need anything more from us?"

The young girl smiled at them both and beckoned for them to join her at the desk.

"All I need you to do is to sign this little slip of paper to say you have vacated the property and you can be on your way home."

The girls looked at one another and smiled weakly, as they thought they had been rumbled and went to join the girl at the reception.

After they had signed the document, they bid their farewells, saying how lovely their stay was and went out towards the car park where the taxi was to meet them.

The fresh air felt good and they did not have long to wait before their taxi appeared and the driver was so different, being young and very polite, heaving their cases into the back without a grumble and opening the doors for them to get in.

He kept up a witty banter on the way to the Station and made them chuckle talking about some of the other drivers and how they were quite grumpy and set in their ways. He took them right up to the entrance and helped them with their cases and this time the girls gave him a generous tip for his trouble. The very smiley young man at this point, thanked them kindly and returned to his cab, driving off with a wave of his hand out of the window.

The girls trundled their cases on to the station and as before there did not seem to be anyone to help them. Anna went into the little hut at the end of the platform but it was empty. Oh well, there were a few people waiting and presumably, the next train would take them to Exeter where they would be able to change trains for Salisbury.

When the crowd started to surge forward they knew the train was on its way and when it had stopped they boarded with the help of a kind gentleman heaving Sandy's case onto the carriage. They quickly found a seat, gave sighs of relief, and settled down for the first part of their journey home. They always found things to chat about and the journey went quickly so before they knew it they were pulling into the station.

They dragged their cases out and looked around for the porters who were supposed to help them but as they feared none were to be seen. They looked at the information board and found that they had to go over to the other side of the track to get their train so, aware that they had little time, went towards the lift at the far end. A few people were also going in that direction and they started to chatter noisily.

The lift disgorged its passengers and they started to walk along the platform towards the train that was sitting there.

Spying a large gentleman quite a way off with a flag and a whistle in his hand they hurried towards him wanting to ask if this was the right train. He started to wave his hands madly and put the whistle to his lips, urging them to get on the train.

They could not hear him but he looked so cross and was about to blow the whistle. They found a door and just piled into it, pushing and shoving their cases aboard. so frightened were they that they would be injured getting on, that they almost fell inside the carriage. The train left immediately and they did not even know if they were on the right one!

Hells bells, if they were wrong then so be it, they were too tired to even care. Luckily the L.E.D sign in the carriage showed that they were indeed on the right train which would eventually end up in London stopping at Salisbury.

Sandy was first to break the silence that had ensued whilst they both caught their breath.

"You know who he was, don't you?"

"No! Who?" said Anna.

"He was the Fat Controller from Thomas the Tank Engine."

Anna really thought she was going to wet her pants there and then as she saw the funny side of it all and just doubled up with uncontrollable laughter. Sandy followed suit and they laughed and giggled for over ten minutes, their eyes streaming with tears, until they could not continue due to the pain around their middles.

Low and behold about thirty minutes later, who should emerge from the doors at the end of the carriage but "the Fat Controller himself." He recognised them and said they should not have dithered on the platform as he had to make sure the train got off on time and then started saying how much money would be lost if they were even as much as a minute late!

Anna looked him square in the eyes and told him that if they had lost their footing they would not be alive to catch his blessed train and, if they had survived, they would have sued him and the company for much more money than if they had been late.

He was not amused and gave them a sickly smile, moving on down the carriage muttering to himself about silly women of a certain age!

Bloody cheek! Sandy felt like following him down the carriage and pushing him off at the next station to see if he liked it!

When he had gone they comforted themselves with a ham sandwich and a drink of fizzy lemonade. It really did all happen to them.

For the rest of the journey they talked in a low key and made plans for when they got home. They would have a cuppa first and then break out the laptop to start their search for Mr Jake Bonham and see just what they could uncover about their 'man of mystery'.

Before long they arrived at Salisbury and made their weary

way towards the car park and the taxi rank.

They were still chuckling as they emerged from the station entrance and were still having trouble controlling Sandy's large, duffle, suitcase, thingy whose wheels did not want to go in the same direction as they were. The stupid thing kept falling over to one side and they would have to heave it upright, before moving on. Giggling and chuckling like a couple of teenagers.

Eva had no trouble spotting them, and her rage grew so fierce that she thought her face would explode it was so hot. Her hands on the steering wheel were clamped tight in the leather gloves she was wearing. She leant forwards and rested her forehead on the steering wheel trying to gain some composure. Pulling herself together and taking deep breaths, Eva raised her beautiful head and watched as the girls made their precarious way towards a waiting taxi. Eventually, the cases were bundled into the back of the cab and the girls scrambled into the back, all arms and legs and handbags.

Eva switched on the ignition and pulled away slowly, keeping her distance from the taxi as she was driving a very bright red Porsche. Damn, she should have brought the Range Rover which, although huge, was not so conspicuous. Too late now, the deed was beginning and she would see it through to their end!

With that little pun made to herself, she smiled nastily and clenched the steering wheel harder as if to gain strength from the action for what wicked deeds lay ahead. Eva never felt fear, only excitement as the adrenalin coursed through her veins like a steam train making her eyes burn brightly in her over-flushed, perfectly made-up face.

The taxi turned into a sort of crescent which lay on a rise and, keeping her distance, Eva observed the two women alighting the vehicle, paying the middle-aged driver and trudging up the path of a house in the middle of a terrace of houses built around a pretty green. They opened the door and waved to the driver dragging their cases in. They must have gone through to the kitchen, possibly at the back, to make a cup of tea. Eva looked at her watch and it was just turning 5 o'clock in the afternoon. Eva looked about her and at the houses and saw that each pair of houses had a side access to the back of the property.

A brilliant stroke of luck for the black deed she was intent on carrying out to rid herself of these two meddling imbeciles. Silently she hunched down in her leather seat, folding her arms and began her long wait until dark.

Sandy and Anna were absolutely beat! They almost fell inside the front door of Sandy's house, left the suitcases where they had plonked them and went straight through to Sandy's pretty kitchen. There they busied themselves with making a really hot pot of tea, buttered some bread, adding jam and chocolate biscuits to the tray. This done they carried it through to the front lounge and silently poured their tea, adding sugar, crunching on biscuits and hoovering up the bread and jam.

They did not converse whilst they were eating this feast and drinking the hot tea as they needed the input of sugar and hot liquid to replenish their ailing energy. Once every scrap was eaten and all the tea was gone they both heaved a simultaneous sigh of contentment and lay back against the cushions of their respective chairs.

They must have fallen asleep as when they started to stir, the light was fading outside. Anna was the first to break the silence with an almighty yawn and a huge stretch, pushing her legs out akimbo in front of her and raising her arms above her head. They say yawns are catching and this must be true as Sandy did exactly the same thing only 30 seconds later!

"Wow, that was just what the doctor ordered, I think we both needed that after what has happened over the last few days," said Sandy.

Anna, nodded her agreement and grinned at her friend, going over and giving her a big hug.

Once they had cleared all the plates and cups of tea and washed everything up they went back to the lounge where Sandy turned on her laptop. They searched for Jake's name and sure enough, a million and one articles shot up on the screen. All about his Company, what he had been up to in the last few months and how he was a "bit of a lad" by all accounts.

Whilst the two girls were deeply involved in their research they did not hear the car come to a halt outside the house. Stealthily, Eva unwound herself from the drivers seat, made sure her gloves were pulled on tight and adjusted the scarf she had placed over her head. Moving like a cat she located the little passage which led to the back of the houses. When she emerged she turned to her right and saw the double glazed back door of the property.

Now, it all rested on the door not having been locked after one of them had taken rubbish out to the bins, as one of the bins was slightly leaning with some paper hanging out of it. Taking the handle in her hand she depressed it and to her delight and amazement the door gave way inwards very silently.

Eva had a torch on her phone and looked around the small, neat kitchen. Just as she had thought there was a gas hob, you could always smell the faint whiff of gas in a house when they used this method of energy. Her luck became even better when she found that the oven was powered by gas also. Quickly she opened the oven door and then turned all the knobs on to full. There was an incessant hissing noise and the pungent smell of gas began to permeate the whole kitchen. Eva quickly turned on her elegant heels and exited the kitchen by way of her entry. She moved quickly down the passage and lowered herself into the sports car.

Eva could not help banging her fists onto the steering wheel and then she cradled her head between her fisted hands, pushing on her temples and shaking her head at the same time. This action gave her immense satisfaction and fed her warped, twisted, ego. She could imagine one of the women going into the kitchen in a half hour's time and switching on the light. Boom! The whole kitchen would explode and they would go up with it! She was now shaking her head from side to side and screeching to herself with utter madness, her eyes burning feverishly in her head. She had taken off her head scarf and shook her blond tresses free, scraping her gloved hands through it to lift it away from her face. So confident was she that this plan would work, that she gunned the engine, not thinking about the noise it would create, and took off at the speed of light, the back end twitching as it took the corner of the green.

From inside the house Sandy had heard the screech of the tyres and the throaty engine noise and was a little perplexed by it as no-one around the crescent had fast cars and they certainly did not drive them irresponsibly as there were sometimes children playing on the green. Sandy went over to the curtains and looked out just catching sight of a bright red Porsche exiting at the bottom of the crescent, just missing a car coming around the corner.

Who, by all that was holy, would be zooming around the crescent at this time of night, in a bright red Porsche? It was definitely a woman, as she had caught sight of long blonde hair trailing behind by the light of the street lamp. Just at that moment Anna started to sniff noisily and said that she thought she could smell something funny. Sandy put two and two together and came up with one thousand! They had looked at hundreds of pictures of Jake over the last hour and during that time had found out that he was married to a very wealthy socialite. Her father owned the business and Jake was a Director. During their search several news articles had flashed up regarding Eva, his wife. One mentioned how, when she was at University, her boyfriend was found dead in his flat, due to an overdose. Eva had been brought in for questioning but never charged with anything. Then years later Eva had married a very good looking man. He came from nowhere and had no wealth to speak of, until he met Eva.

He had died in very suspicious circumstances whilst on their yacht in Italy. Again, Eva had been questioned, but the police concluded that he had had too much to drink that night at a party, slipped and fell, drowning before anyone had noticed he was missing. In the same article there was a picture of Eva with her father and she certainly did not look very distraught about the untimely death of her husband. In several of the pictures she was pictured leaning against a bright, red, Porsche AND she had long blond hair! Oh my God! What was Eva… Jake's wife, doing outside her house? Oh my God! That WAS bloody gas they could smell and it WAS coming from her Kitchen.

As quickly as she could she grabbed Anna, motioned towards the kitchen and mouthed the word GAS! Anna's eyes opened wide and her shoulders went up but by this time Sandy had pulled her towards the front door, telling her to get her laptop and bag and just get out as quickly as possible. Sandy and Anna scrambled out of the front of the house and then Sandy made a mobile 999 phone call to the police telling them as much as she could as to why she thought something very suspicious was going on. The police told her to raise the alarm with her neighbours as quickly as possible in case there was a gas leak, and get them all out of their properties and as far away down the crescent as possible. They would notify the fire brigade and the ambulance service, just in case!

As quickly as their legs would carry them, Sandy and Anna, flew to each house in turn, knocking on their doors and making them aware of the situation. They told everyone to check their houses to see that everyone was accounted for and not to leave anyone inside, then get as far away from the crescent as possible, to the other side of the green. Anna and Sandy were shivering, not from the cold, but from the terrifying fright they both felt. All at once it seemed there was complete pandemonium and utter confusion as people spilled out of their houses, in different modes of attire. Children were mostly in their pyjamas and their parents had wrapped them in blankets to keep them warm.

People were shouting and gesticulating, babies were crying and mothers shouting for their older children to keep close and not wander. Dad's were herding their little families down to the bottom of the green where they were all huddled together, waiting for the services to arrive. They were asking Sandy and Anna what had happened and, without alarming them too much, Sandy just said she had smelled the gas and thought it best to just exit the houses until help arrived.

They all stood and watched the blue lights approach, and heard the sirens wailing, as first the police cars arrived, closely followed by the Fire Brigade and then the ambulance. They all came to an abrupt halt, the blue lights flashing madly. One police officer stood in front of the crowd and shouted out Sandy's name. Sandy moved forward and made herself known describing quickly what they had seen and heard and what they suspected. The officer raised an eyebrow, as if not quite believing her brief description of the last few days, but he was more interested in people's safety and how they could move these people to the little scout hut not far away, where at least they would be warm and hopefully there would be a kitchen of sorts in order to make tea or coffee.

The police guided the crowd down to the little hut and officers went door to door to see if everyone was evacuated.

The fire brigade had located the gas main and were in the process of turning off the gas. There seemed to be firemen everywhere and they went round the back of the house. They had full breathing gear on with masks when they entered the back door. They had a meter with them that measured the amount of gas present, glowing bright red if it was above safe levels, which it did! It was not until the levels dropped and a green light came on that they entered the building to turn off the appliances.

It seemed ages before one of the firemen emerged from the side passage, removing his mask and waving his arms above his head then giving the thumbs-up sign. A little cheer went up from those not in the scout hut and they went to inform the others what had happened. The families were told not to go back to their houses straight away as the firemen would make sure all the appliances were safe.

Over two hour later, everyone was finally allowed to go back to their homes and they thanked all the firemen and police for their prompt response and how they had handled the situation. Many new friends had been made over cups of tea in the scout hut and they were all glad the dangerous situation had been resolved safely.

8:

Big Mistake!

Eva had taken off with the speed of light, a woman possessed, she could feel the adrenaline rising within her. When she got like this she felt so alive, every cell in her body was tingling with excitement she thought of the huge explosion back at the house and how both women would be wiped from her life and out of her hair. She was approaching the Motorway now and glanced in the mirror as she joined the fast-moving traffic and caught sight of her distorted features the hatred had etched onto her beautiful face. Only Eva did not see the distortion, she saw the increased blood flow to her already flushed cheeks and the over bright blue eyes. A slow smile drifted across her face as an almighty contented sigh escaped her. By God she was awesome, she was incredible, she would phone Jake and get him to grovel at her feet. Without her and her Father's fortune he was nothing but a small, floundering fish in a little pond. However, he was very handsome and very good in bed, she could not argue with that so, for the moment, he could stay around.

Eva had been driving on automatic pilot but had not been watching her speed and did not see the flash of the camera as she was caught on a particularly notorious stretch of the Motorway with multiple speed changes due to endless roadworks. No matter to Eva really, as the fine would be but a nuisance and Daddy would make it all go away. Big Mistake!

The firemen had finished checking everything and the ambulance had long since left, only the police remained and were all over Sandy's property, checking for fingerprints or any other clue as to who had been in their property that evening. The two women had to answer a whole load of questions as to whether they had indeed left the gas on but, even the chief inspector had to agree that they would not have turned all the burners on and the oven, leaving the door open as well. They were asked about what had happened on their holiday and why they suspected the mysterious man. Anna told them about what she saw on the night he dragged something out of the chalet and they recounted the incident along the dangerous wall and their rescue. The police listened to everything and said they had spoken to Jake that day, and he had explained about his various business meetings and how he had been taken ill and spent a couple of days in bed, so did not see the news or answer his phone, not knowing they wanted to get in touch with him. The girls told them about how he had threatened them and how scared they were but could see from the looks passing from one officer to another, that they were not being taken seriously enough. They also told them about the purse, phone and keys they had found hidden in the tunnel, the police said they would check this out also.

It had been a very long day and after taking down all their notes the police left saying they would get back to them. Anna looked at Sandy and shrugged her shoulders.

"I do not think they believe us Sandy and think we are a couple of bored women trying to get some cheap thrills and excitement" Sandy looked at her friend and nodded her head in agreement.

"I know, it is so frustrating, we sound so lame. It is a very tall story for anyone to swallow, I would not really believe it myself if I had not witnessed it first hand."

"The trouble is I think Eva is totally nuts and she thinks she has blown us to smithereens but what is she going to do when she finds out we are still alive?"

Eva had arrived home and sat for a while in the drive of her huge plush mansion, she was so wired at the moment that she had to de-escalate her rising emotions. Everything was going around in her head and she was taken back to when she met Catherine at the chalet. How she hated her, how she loathed her. When Catherine had recovered from her shock at seeing Eva, she had started to mouth off and shout the odds at Eva unsuspectingly thrusting her angry face against Eva's distorted one. She did not see Eva grasp the heavy glass paperweight that was on the coffee table, pinning the brochures beneath its glassy weight. She did not heed the warning glint in her stunningly beautiful but cold, hard, eyes, or see the flash of the paperweight as Eva smashed it against her temple. Abruptly her shouting ceased and, for a heart-stopping moment, she hovered there whilst her face went ashen and her eyes opened wide as if trying to comprehend what had happened. Catherine made a grabbing motion towards Eva, her hands flailing uncontrollably. Then, thud, crack, she had gone down hard and hit her head on the marble mantle as she fell.

Silence!

Nothing!

She did not even twitch.

Total oblivion.

Eva had watched it unfold before her as in slow motion drinking in the agony she had seen on the wretched girl's horror-stricken face.

Oh my! That felt good!

Eva could feel the hot blood racing to her face and she swept her hand across it feeling the scorching heat. She looked down at her other hand still holding the paperweight, limply dangling from her fingers and saw the bright red blood dripping from it.

Suddenly Eva took hold of herself. Thankfully the bitch had landed on the large rug in front of the fireplace and the blood from her head was seeping onto it. Likewise, where she was standing the drips from the paperweight were also caught on the rug.

Taking stock of the situation she had to clean up the paperweight then get rid of it. She would leave straight away as Jake would be here soon and he could clear up this mess, as he always did. Eva carefully made her way across to the kitchen area and located some kitchen roll. Holding the weight under the tap she washed the smattering of blood away, carefully wrapping it in several sheets of paper. This done, she popped it in her pocket then checked outside to see if anyone was about and finding it all clear, quickly exited the chalet and walked quickly down the path to the car park. On her way she saw a green rubbish bin, excellent, she opened the top, fished out the parcel and threw it forcefully into its belly, watching it being swallowed up by the rest of the rubbish lying within. Eva did not appreciate the evil smell wafting up to her delicate nostrils and speedily found her car, climbed in and slowly drew away, so as not to draw any attention to herself.

Eva's face had taken on a glazed look as she recalled all this and a slow smile covered her face.

Slowly she returned to the present and gave herself a shake, no time to reminisce now she had to call Jake. If the police had finished with him they could fly to Italy and stay on the yacht for a while, the enormity of what she had done did not even register on the Richter scale and in Eva's world, all was well.

9:

The Best Laid Plans

Jake was downing a 'straight' whiskey, he felt clammy and hot as he had been at the police station a good part of the day answering their stupid questions and going over everything again and again. Eventually, they seemed satisfied and had let him go. God, he needed a shower and a change of clothes but he had to have his stiff drink first to steady his jangled nerves.

Just then he heard the front door open and Eva appeared in the lounge door, she had a brittleness about her and looked more stunning than ever just standing, framed in the doorway, smiling broadly at him, head on one side.

"I can do with one of those, darling, although on second thoughts make it a G & T, a large one."

Eva peeled her gloves off one by one and then let her coat drop on the floor as she swayed over to where Jake sat, hunched forward, his drink between his hands, the ice chinking up the sides of the glass.

He looked up warily and then stood up to fetch Eva her drink, as it was easier to do that than refuse. Eva watched him pour the gin into a cut glass, pour the tonic, add the ice from the bucket and add a slice. This done he handed her the drink, arm outstretched.

Eva moved forward to accept the glass but, in doing so, she clasped his hand over the glass and pulled it and him towards her scarlet mouth. It was as if he was in slow motion and he watched as she put the glass to her lips, with his hand still clasped around it and then drank deeply, her eyes never leaving his stunned face.

Once she had taken her fill she pulled him towards her and clasped him around the neck, the glass forgotten and dropped to the carpeted floor, where luckily it did not shatter. As Eva so often did, she moved her smooth face over his stubble weary one. He tried to pull away but she was having none of it! Insidiously she nuzzled into him and he could smell her provocatively expensive perfume fill his flaring nostrils. God, he needed a shower but as always his body and mind were weak and Eva did something to him when she was like this, as in a trance, she pulled him down on top of her to the sofa. He could feel his arousal and even though he had experienced such a shitty day, was dog tired and grubby, he could not refuse the call of his pathetic body and began to remove his jacket, slowly pulling away from her. Immediately, she reached out for him again and forced his head down to her ample cleavage.

Jake was completely lost and within minutes had stripped himself and her to their bare essentials. They both liked to keep some articles of underwear on as this seemed to heighten the passion. They tumbled onto the floor and rolled this way and that, her tongue found the soft lobe of his ear and she licked and sucked until he was totally mindless. In his turn he pulled out her ivory, plump breasts from the fine wisps of lace covering them and took first one, and then the other, into his waiting mouth.

Eva started to wail and claw at his back, her own body arching towards him slick and moist, urging him to find and conquer her very molten core.

Jake could take no more and entered Eva, after pushing her non-existent briefs to one side, with such a forceful thrust that she cried out and caught hold of his hair pulling, until he cried out also, clasping his large hands over hers and pulling her away from his head. They were both on fire and at the same moment experienced a simultaneous climax that had them panting and gasping, rolling and writhing, arms, legs, hands, mouths clawing and kneading until they both started to climb down from the frantic vortex they had created, to drop spent, and moist against the long, soft carpet.

How long they stayed there neither knew but Jake was the first to move as he extricated himself from the jumble of limbs, hearing her soft moans and sighs. He moved wearily towards the stairs and ultimately the bathroom where he could now have that urgent shower which might, if he was lucky, clear his jumbled head.

Boy, Eva was on fire this time, was this making up sex or had she been up to something?

Jake never knew with Eva but what he did know was it was amazing and he could not refuse her.

Eva felt Jake leave and knew she would also have to make her way to bed, a slow smile crossed her beautiful face and she stretched luxuriously extending her lovely arms above her head. In the morning she would scan the news for the demise of those two stupid creatures just the thought of it gave her a buzz and she could feel her body tingle with electric impulses stirring her senses.

Unbeknown to Anna and Sandy, the police had taken them

seriously and the following morning, had arrived in Devon and followed up on the information they had given them.

Early the next morning, Anna was humming to herself after her shower and on her way down to the kitchen to make a cup of tea, when her mobile rang. Anna saw it was from her husband and quickly answered it. He was on his way to a meeting which had been called unexpectedly and advised her to stay with Sandy for another couple of days, if she would have her! Cheeky! Anna assured him it would be fine and that she would see him soon when he had completed his trip, telling him to be careful and not to get too tired. Grumbling that she fussed too much they exchanged air kisses and rang off.

Over breakfast the two friends were discussing what they could get up to together during this extended holiday as Sandy had said that, of course, it was ok to stay for a while longer. They were planning what they were going to eat and if they would take a trip into town for, you guessed it, shopping, when the phone rang. Sandy answered and it was the Police. Anna sat next to her on the sofa and listened in to the conversation. The Police had followed up their story and could affirm that they now had a forensic squad, checking out the chalet and the surrounding area. They had scoured the place under the old tunnel and had found a phone, purse and keys as they had described. The phone was clean and the sim card removed, the purse was empty and the keys contained house keys and car keys. They had questioned the reception staff at the holiday park and a car had been parked there for a few days which did not belong to any of the occupants of the holiday lets and they were about to get it towed. The keys they found opened the car and it was registered to a Catherine

Dubois! This now meant that Catherine was in the vicinity of the chalet and the girl's story was starting to make a lot of sense. The police were not discounting them now as two silly older women but taking them very seriously indeed.

In fact, the detective in charge of the case, asked them both to think carefully about what they had seen and, if they remembered anything that might be relevant, to let them know immediately. He rang off telling Sandy they would be in touch shortly with any update on the ongoing investigation but to meanwhile not say a word to anyone, as it could harm the case if any details were leaked at this crucial time.

"Well this is exciting, sort of," said Sandy and visibly shuddered as she realised that this was indeed a murder enquiry and Catherine Dubois was possibly dead and they had been witnesses to her body being concealed somewhere nearby. Anna nodded and pulled a wry face.

"Yes, dear friend, our little holiday escape to dear little Devon, was more dangerous than we could ever have imagined."

Anna walked over to Sandy and they hugged each other soundly, taking solace from each other and much-needed reassurance.

10:

Hell Hath No Fury!

Eva awoke, opened her lovely eyes and let consciousness wash over her slowly. Glancing at the bedside clock she saw it was still fairly early, so she threw back her sumptuous duvet and silk sheets, pushed her bare feet into her slippers and sauntered to the bathroom for a long hot shower. Humming softly to herself Eva showered and dressed, put on her makeup, pulling strange faces into her illuminated mirror, plucking a few wayward eyebrow strands and finishing with a gleaming lip gloss. Looking at her reflection she smiled and did a small curtsey to herself, pleased with what she saw and knowing she was very attractive, finished with a pouty kiss planted on her fingers and thrown to her image in recognition of her high self-esteem.

Making her way down the carpeted stairs to the entrance hall and then along to the kitchen, she picked up her iPad and began to fire it up as she walked. Kettle filled and switched on, bread in the toaster and depressed, she sat down at the marble island in the middle of the room, flipped open her tablet and searched for the news. Eva was absolutely certain she would see huge headlines about a big explosion at a house in Salisbury where two women had met their demise but, to her chagrin, even though she searched thoroughly, there was nothing.

Using the search engine, she searched for the online local

Salisbury paper, and found a small article which explained about the services being called to a semi-detached house where a gas leak was suspected. The neighbourhood had been evacuated and the fire brigade had dealt with the emergency. After thoroughly checking the area, everyone was allowed back to their homes after a couple of hours.

"Damn! Damn! and Double Damn!" Eva's face was contorted with white-hot fury, they had got away with it, they were alive, but how? Clever bitches, lucky cows who has that kind of luck? Obviously, they did! The blasphemies that came out of Eva's mouth turned the air purple, blue and black. Suddenly, the phone rang in the hall and she heard Jake answer. He had still been in bed when she got up and must have now showered and dressed for work. She heard him raise his voice and then the phone was banged back on its holder and he came thundering into the kitchen.

"The bloody police want me in for more questioning as they have turned up new evidence, apparently, and are on their way now to take me to the station. What bloody evidence, there is none, I saw to that and covered my tracks damn well, they are just being morons and chucking their weight around as they need their quota for the week!" Jake looked at Eva and his face was tight with anger, his eyes like flints.

"We are going to have to shelve our plans to leave the country on the Jet as they are banning me from all travel until further notice. What the hell is going on here, they seemed fine when they spoke to me last and were totally satisfied with my story and alibi as to where I had been, so what has changed now?"

As Jake was speaking a huge police car drew up in front of the house and two officers alighted.

"Well, Jake, your day is going to be fun, lover, just go with it and answer all their stupid questions, we will still leave the country when they have decided to drop the case, which they will do."

Eva pushed up from her stool by the island and walked over to him winding her arms around his neck and looking him straight in his angry eyes, "Remember this, my darling and don't be long."

Eva took possession of Jakes mouth and urged his lips apart, rubbing her body against him and flicking her tongue in and out of his willing mouth. Jake responded and gathered her against him, grazing her full lips with his teeth in a challenging gesture. At last, pulling away, as the doorbell sounded, he muttered, "hold that thought for Italy my firebrand."

Once the police and Jake had left in a flurry of warnings, and red tape, Eva's mind began to turn once again

to the two women, the thorns in her side. If Jake was in the shit then she would let him take the rap, he was too weak and spineless anyway, she would make sure they did not suspect her and would lay the blame firmly with Jake.

Eva arrived at Sandy's house and rang the bell, she did not have to wait long before it was pulled open and heard a soft gasp come from Sandy and then Anna as the door was opened more fully. Eva had several grazes and bruises on her face and asked if she could come in to have a word with them about Jake.

"I wanted to explain," said Eva as she sat down in the soft chair in Sandy's lounge.

"I followed you back to your house the other night as I was worried Jake was going to try something, I parked near your house and kept watch for a while as Jake's car was not there. You were both visible in your lounge talking, so I waited for quite a long time, until it got dark in fact, but he did not appear, therefore I left thinking that you were fine and that he had not gone ahead with his plan to hurt you."

Eva gestured towards her bruised and battered face and then started to cry.

"He did this to me this morning as I found out that he had visited you and is going to try and put the blame on me. He is a very manipulative and sadistic man and is saying all sorts of horrible things about me, I hope they lock him up and throw away the key."

Anna and Sandy were totally taken in by Eva's brilliant performance and tried to comfort her. Anna offered her some tissues and went looking for more in her coat pocket. As she came into the room with the small travel pack, something fell on the floor and Eva immediately stopped her crying and stared at the jewelled lipstick case, rolling, glistening and glinting across the carpeted floor, to come to rest by her feet, clearly displaying the initials CD. Eva was transfixed by the case and slowly raised her eyes to Anna.

"What a lovely lipstick case, and so unusual, where did you get it?"

Anna retrieved the gold case and popped it on the coffee table in front of Eva.

"I found it on the path by the chalets, broken and battered and was going to hand it into Reception but with all that was happening, it totally slipped my mind." However, I suppose it is evidence now and I will have to hand it in. Eva nodded and slowly turned her head towards them.

"What was it that you saw Jake doing that got him so angry?"

Anna and Sandy recounted what they had seen as they had totally fallen for Eva's 'little girl lost' and 'poor me' story. As they recalled their story, Anna suddenly remembered when Jake had buried something by the rocks before he had gone along the wall.

She turned to Sandy, "We must ring the police tomorrow and tell them about this, I don't expect it is significant but it is what made us suspicious of him in the first place. He seemed to be heeling something in with his foot and it was above the waterline, so most probably would not have been washed away. We must also tell them about the lipstick case which I had entirely forgotten about."

Eva listened to all they had to say very intently and made the appropriate shocked facial expressions with a few audible gasps and "How awful" "No!" and "Really."

"I suspected he was up to something but nothing has prepared me for this!"

Eva started to cry again, very softly, for a while and then dabbed at her eyes and blew her nose delicately, visibly shaking herself in front of their eyes as if trying to pull herself together.

"I must get going as I have taken up too much of your time already, Jake is at the Police Headquarters now as they pulled him in this morning saying they had more evidence. It will be interesting to see what he says to them about me to try and save his miserable skin."

Eva made to get up from her chair and as she did so dropped her bag on the floor spilling the contents on the carpet. The two girls rushed to help and amidst all the confusion Eva deftly swiped the lipstick case from the coffee table and shoved it into the pocket of her coat. A short while later, the contents of her bag retrieved and scooped back into its interior, Eva took her leave of them in a flurry of Guess cream leather-gloved handshakes, Hermes chiffon scarf and a waft of Chanel perfume. Then she was gone, leaving the two girls feeling sorry for her being married to a man like Jake, who was obviously a maniac, after seeing the evidence of what he had done to her that morning! The girls walked back into the lounge and retrieved the used crockery and cleared the coffee table. It was then that Sandy noticed the lipstick case was missing and looked on the floor and under the table for it. Scratching her head slightly and looking perplexed, she asked Anna if she had perhaps moved it. Shaking her head Anna proceeded to the kitchen to deposit the used cups in the sink for washing. Over her shoulder as she left the room she caught Sandy's eye and, with realisation dawning on them both, simultaneously they knew they had been played. Anna came slowly back into the lounge her face perplexed. "What did Eva want with the lipstick case, unless she had recognised it and, thinking back, she could not tear her eyes away when it rolled onto the floor from the pack of tissues." She had pumped them for information and like complete idiots they had played into her hands. However, what good would it do her as the Police were, at this moment, questioning Jake and all the evidence pointed to him, however the niggles persisted.

Eva drove home like a maniac, her mind would not stop turning this way and that, yes, she had the lipstick case but what had Jake hidden in the sand? When she was really troubled Eva would play with the pendant her Father had given her many years ago, like a string of worry beads. She took her hand off the wheel and felt for the necklace, running her free hand round her neck. Placing both hands on the wheel she realised, too late, it was not there and, come to think of it, she had not felt its presence for a few days. Strange, she nearly always wore it day and night, unless she was going somewhere special and put on one of her diamond necklaces.

Eva swerved violently as realisation suddenly poured in, she gained control of the car and could feel the blood draining from her face. She had to pull off the road and spotting a sign for the next services took that exit and came to a halt in the large car park. Crumbling visibly, she leant forward over the steering wheel, her head thumping, her heart racing. My God! How had she not remembered, that when Catherine fell, after she had hit her, her flailing arms had caught at the chain around her neck and she had snapped it off as she fell backwards to the floor. Eva had felt no pain as she was too fired up to notice and was only concerned with exiting the scene of the crime as quickly as her stilettoed feet would accommodate her! Hell and damnation, what was she going to do? If, as she suspected, Jake had stupidly hidden her locket in the sand, those two meddling cretins were going to tell them about what they had seen and they would retrieve it. It had her initials on it, it had Catherine's fingerprints on it and it had her bloody fingerprints on it with oodles of DNA from all concerned. Crap! Crap! Crap! she pummeled the poor unsuspecting steering wheel, tore at her beautiful blonde hair and stamped her feet on the pedals which, although it hurt she did not even flinch.

This morning she thought she had it all wrapped up, bruising her own face, which was no mean feat! Playing the poor, hard done by wife and stacking things up against Jake was her sole purpose and to get those two stupid bitches feeling sorry for her. However, she was totally f****d! Firstly, the lipstick case and secondly the locket which was the totally crappy role of the crap dice! Eva moved forwards and placed her bent arm on the steering wheel and leant over it, butting against herself time after time in a bid to think. What should she do now? She had to retrieve the locket, she had to! Trouble was they were going to phone the Police in the morning which narrowed her options dramatically, she only had a few hours in which to try and find whatever Jake had buried, hopefully the locket, and get back to London. Also she had to be very careful not to be seen.

She would travel down dressed in dark outdoor gear, waterproof boots and armed with a trowel and a torch. The women had given her a really good description of where to search and it was above the waterline. If she arrived just before dawn she could locate the article and make it back to London before anyone suspected.

Now she had a plan, Eva was totally wired and driving out of the services and onto the Motorway, made her way towards London, her house and a change of clothes, ready for the exhumation!

Anna and Sandy did not feel good about Eva's visit and were very mistrusting after the disappearance of the lipstick case, as only she could have taken it! Rather than phoning the Police in the morning they decided to phone them there and then, telling them what had occurred and their gut reaction that something was not right.

They were patched straight through to the detective in charge of the case and he listened quietly to all they had to say. He seemed to be in deep thought as he did not answer them for quite a while, and when he did, it was to inform them that Jake had been formally charged. They had impounded Jake's car and forensics had been over it with a fine-tooth comb. Jake had obviously had it washed and valeted, however luckily for them, the garage had been a little sloppy and had not completely cleaned under the wheel arches. Minute splashes of clay-like soil were found and it had prompted them to look for somewhere nearby, like an old quarry, which had that type of soil. Bingo! A disused quarry had been discovered and samples of the clay had been taken and matched with the spatterings taken from Jake's car. They were now in the process of dredging the deep lake at the bottom of the quarry. The detective was pretty certain that a body would be discovered and it did not take a genius to put all the evidence together and for Jake to be firmly in the frame. They were also searching the whole area for evidence and the entire Holiday Park was being searched, including the rubbish bins, which had not been emptied since the incident! Now that Anna and Sandy had told them of their suspicions regarding Eva they were going to delve deeper into her past and see what they turned up! They thanked the girls and asked them to get in touch if they remembered anything else which could be relevant to the case. They were also going to send a surveillance car to be positioned outside of the house in case Eva returned, just a precaution they said!

Anna looked at Sandy and they did not have to say a word as they knew what danger they had been in and possibly were still in, during the last few days. When they were faced with such dangerous circumstances they did what any self-respecting women would do, they put the kettle on for a hot, sweet, cup of tea!

EB

11:

Gotcha!

Eva arrived at the house and swiftly climbed the long sweep of elegant stairs two at a time. A quick shower, then dress in the clothes she was quickly taking from her walk-in wardrobe and drawers. Searching through her footwear she found a pair of waterproof boots and donned black skinny jeans, a charcoal sweater and a waterproof coat. On her bright head she rammed on a black ski-hat. Surveying herself in the mirror she was pleased with the result and ran down the stairs and into the hall. Making sure she had a stout trowel from the garden and a waterproof bag she exited the house and slammed the front door. As usual Eva took energy from this situation and was sure what she was about to do would clear her completely and Jake would be firmly in the frame. Poor sod! He was just another slave to her every whim and although he was good looking in a rugged way and good in bed, she would find another, younger, model to take his place. With that thought she smiled broadly, stuffed everything into the Range Rover, just one of her many vehicles, and slowly turned out of the drive. Slowly. Slowly, catchee monkey, with this thought her laugh turned into a cackle and she dropped her chin down low on her chest luxuriating in her own brilliance.

Eva had the sound system full-on in the car and was singing along with her favourite heavy metal music, every so often she would catch a glimpse of herself in the mirror whilst checking the road and her eyes were wild with excitement. It was going to be a long drive but would be worth the effort when she was on her yacht, stretched out in the blazing sun sipping her Singapore sling. Oh, yes she could feel the heat and the sea breeze as she tapped her thumbs on the steering wheel to the beat.

Eventually, Eva arrived at the seafront and, at the moment it was pitch black however, she checked her watch, it would start to get light fairly soon. Parking the car, she opened the back door and took out the heavy-duty torch and trowel, and put them in a small backpack, snatched up the bag of sandwiches and got back in the front seat.

As she began to eat the sandwiches Eva realised she was indeed very hungry and had not had anything to eat since this morning. Eating the sandwiches, she washed them down with several long gulps of water from a fresh bottle she always kept in the car. Feeling much better and more alert, she checked her watch and took stock of where she was. Getting out of the car she hunched into the backpack and switched on her torch, making sure there was no one around. Moving swiftly she arrived at the steps down to the beach and as luck would have it, the tide was far out anyway thus making her mission much easier. There was the sign the women had mentioned with directions to Dawlish Warren and there was the outcrop of rocks they also described.

Carefully, Eva made her way down the stone steps, the powerful torch illuminating her way. The fingers of light were just beginning to creep over the seascape and shapes were becoming clearer. Dropping down onto her haunches Eva put the back pack down and took out the trowel. At the base of the rock, she began to dig. This could take forever if Jake had buried the missing locket deeply, she just hoped he had not had the time to do a good job. Fifteen minutes passed and it was getting lighter now, nothing had been revealed and she was quite a way around the outcrop. Suddenly she spotted something, a cream cord sticking out of the disturbed sand.

With her bare hands she clawed at the gritty sand and felt something underneath her fingers. Pulling the exposed cord, a cloth bag was visible and came to the surface. Eva could feel her heart beating wildly, as this looked promising and could be what she was searching for. Sitting back on her heels she undid the bag and felt inside, sure enough there was something inside which she grabbed and withdrew carefully. With an evil smile on her beautiful face, she held the locket aloft, dangling from her immaculately manicured hand, threw her head back and laughed out loud!

Suddenly, there were bright penetrating lights on her face, then lots of noise and the sand was thrown everywhere, the sound of helicopter blades could be heard and a voice barking orders.

"Stay right where you are."

"Don't move"

"Put your hands on your head."

Eva was totally confused and blazingly angry all at once. Shrieking and spitting obscenities, it took both officers to grab her flailing arms and legs to subdue her.

"You bastards, get… off… me, take your filthy hands, away… from… me!

Do you know who I am, you ridiculous morons?

You will pay for this. My Father will utterly destroy you and your bloody incompetent police force."

The whole scene was unreal, like something out of a movie and Anna and Sandy watching from a safe distance were utterly transfixed. They saw what Eva was truly like and both shuddered and hugged each other tightly for moral support, as they now really knew how much danger they had truly been in. Anna's husband was holding both girls within the circle of his arms, as he had been contacted and put in the picture the previous evening and had driven them down to where the police were setting a trap for Eva. He had been worried and cross that Anna had not told him what had happened but quickly forgot all that when he knew they were both safe. The police now had the locket and it would be screened for evidence of fingerprints and DNA.

Eva was almost dragged, kicking and screaming up the stone steps by two burly officers and bundled unceremoniously into the waiting police car. They had to stop several times to warn her not to try and bite or scratch the officers and to bodily haul her up from the promenade where she kept flinging herself. It was a truly pathetic sight and it did not do her any favours at all. Eventually they had her stowed in the back of the car with a police officer either side.

The detective in charge walked over to where Anna, her husband and Sandy were standing, huddled together to try and ward off the images they had just witnessed.

"Thank you for coming and identifying the exact place you saw Jake bury the item. It took great courage and it made our job a lot easier. I have just had a call from the quarry where they have been dredging the lake and they have found a body, which we believe will prove to be that of Catherine Dubois. Added to this Jake is now squealing like a stuck pig and as you'd have guessed, is now telling us the true story of how it was Eva who killed Catherine albeit, she says, accidentally, which will have to be proved in court, and he got rid of the body and did her dirty work for her. We will also look for any evidence proving where she was the night of the gas incident, as her red Porsche is not exactly inconspicuous! I think this will become a major investigation, spanning a long period of time, into the circumstances of how, first her boyfriend and then her husband met their demise. This is, by no means, an open and shut case and, of course, we will need to call on you for your eye witness accounts and you will definitely be called to testify in Court when the time comes."

Anna's husband hugged them soundly within the circle of his outstretched arms and they both smiled at the detective weakly, nodding their weary heads in the affirmative.

After shaking hands, the detective got in the police car and it moved swiftly away, taking Eva back to the Station where she would now be formally charged with Murder, whilst Jake would be charged with accessory to that murder. Both would be looking at severe sentences, especially Eva depending on what other evidence the police uncovered.

Anna's husband moved them forward and said, 'I think this calls for a full English Breakfast at the nearest café, don't you?" and he encompassed them both with a broad grin.

They both nodded and smiled at each other behind his broad back and winked.

"Here's to our next mini-break Anna and who knows, to our

next exciting adventure!"

Whereupon both girls laughed and hurried to catch up Mitchell's retreating figure, honing in on his well-earned breakfast!

As if on queue, Mitchell turned and grinned at them.

"Come on you two, our Brunch is getting cold, last one pays," and he took off like a rocket along the prom.

THE END

OR IS IT?

About the Author

My name is Anne-Marie Sassoli and I was born and grew up in the Cathedral City of Salisbury in Wiltshire. My dear Father was a musician and my Mother worked in the family business, she also loved writing and taught me how to appreciate the written word, how to write stories and compose poetry.

I attended drama school and passed many speech and drama exams and was asked to go to London to become a speech and drama teacher but, unfortunately, my parents could not afford to send me.

I went to a very modern, in those days, secondary school and then on to Business College. I worked as a secretary until I had my daughter in 1977. After I had my son in 1985, I became a vocalist with my Father's dance band and worked with him and my brother, until dad's retirement when he was 80!

I have always written poems, stories and articles and when work and home commitments allowed, I published my first book, *Go Back For Love*, in 2019.

My hobbies are writing and reading books, singing, music, and cruising! I adore Italy and go there whenever possible with my Italian husband and my lovely family.

Acknowledgements

Firstly, I would like to thank dear Sandy, my inspiration, who I lost suddenly, only weeks before publishing this book, for believing in me and being a true friend.

My next thank you, is for my brilliant, darling daughter, Cherie, who is my guide and manager! This brings me to Cherie's husband, Andrew Sassoli-Walker who, so professionally, provided the pictures inside my book. (www.solentphotographer.com)

Lastly, my dear friend Lesley, who helped me so much to carry on writing and even recorded some of this story on her mobile phone, whilst on a bus to, you guessed it, Salisbury!

www.mtp.agency

www.facebook.com/mtp.agency

@mtp_agency

Printed in Great Britain
by Amazon